THE SILENT SHORE

Recent Titles by Rosemary Aitken
available from Severn House Large Print

STORMY WATERS

THE SILENT SHORE

Rosemary Aitken

Severn House Large Print
London & New York

This first large print edition published in Great Britain 2002 by
SEVERN HOUSE LARGE PRINT BOOKS LTD of
9-15, High Street, Sutton, Surrey, SM1 1DF.
First world regular print edition published 2001 by
Severn House Publishers, London and New York.
This first large print edition published in the USA 2002 by
SEVERN HOUSE PUBLISHERS INC., of
595 Madison Avenue, New York, NY 10022

British Library Cataloguing in Publication Data

Aitken, Rosemary
    The silent shore - Large print ed.
    1.   Great Britain - History - George V, 1910 – 1936 - Fiction
    2.   Love stories
    3.   Large type books
    I.   Title
    823.9'14 [F]

    ISBN 0-7278-7199-4

Printed and bound in Great Britain by
MPG Books Ltd, Bodmin, Cornwall.

To Rob and Chris,
who knew about boats
and saved me at least from
the worst mistakes

PART ONE

July – August 1911

One

It was a grey summer day, with a sharp little wind blowing, whisking up the dust from the pavements and bending the branches of the two tired plane trees in the central patch of grass that the residents of Lypiatt Square rather grandly called 'the gardens'. Sprat Nicholls, coming down the steps of number 17, pulled her cape a little closer around her shoulders and shivered.

Megan, the maid from the flat downstairs, was out polishing the knocker and grinned at her as she passed. 'London too draughty for you, is it? I would've thought you'd have been used to a bit of wind, down in your Cornish cove, look.'

Sprat laughed ruefully, but there was a certain truth in the words. Back at Penvarris Cove it could 'blow up dreadful', as Ma used to say, but there was something about the wind in London, the way it sneaked round corners and blew dirt in your eyes, that made a good stiff Atlantic breeze seem almost friendly in comparison.

'Just out to get some hatpins and a paper for Miss Raeburn,' she said by way of reply. 'Morrison's shop she said – is that left or right out of the square? Been here two weeks and I never can remember.'

'Left at the end, down to the corner and straight over, isn't it?' Megan said. 'And watch on the main road, there's been a march down there this morning – these blooming dockers, look – and there's policemen swarming everywhere.'

'Well, I aren't doing any harm, am I?' Sprat said. 'Just running errands for Miss Raeburn, and looking after her like I'm paid to do. Who's going to pay any attention to me?'

Megan giggled. 'Well, somebody's paying attention to you right now,' she said. 'See that fair-haired boy on the cart over there, look? Can't take his eyes off you – and he's had that cart twice around the square already. Coming round again, isn't it?'

'Don't be daft,' Sprat said, 'he never is.' But he was, and she found herself flushing all the same. She was beginning to get accustomed to grinning errand boys whistling at her in the street, and tradesmen, everyone from the knife grinder to the rag-and-bone merchant, calling after her appreciatively. Megan didn't seem to mind it – came all over giggly when the milkman's boy ogled and whistled at her as he ladled

10

the milk into her jug in the morning – but it made Sprat uncomfortable. You never got that sort of thing back home in the Cove. Everybody knew everybody there, that's why – and somebody's father would soon have stepped out and put a stop to any such nonsense.

'Yes here he is, look,' Megan said, with an arch glance. 'Taken a liking to you, Mina.'

Megan called her 'Mina' (short for Wilhemina, awful name!) because Sprat had never revealed her nickname to anyone, not even to Megan, who was her only friend and as much as a stranger here as she was. Miss Raeburn – and anyone else who spoke to her – simply called her 'Nicholls'. The name 'Sprat' belonged to the Cove – it had been Pa's name for her: 'no bigger 'n a sprat' – and she had left it behind when she came to London. Left it behind, along with Denzil Vargo and her shattered dreams.

'That boy's thinking to speak to you, by the look of it,' Megan said gleefully.

'Well, he's got another think coming then,' Sprat retorted. 'Got work to do, haven't I?' And she set off purposefully across the square, leaving Megan to her polishing.

'Here, you! Miss!'

So Megan had been right. Sprat did not look round. She had learned that much in her short stay in London. She raised her head defiantly and walked a little faster.

11

'Miss! Over here!'

She crossed the road deliberately, dodging a hansom cab and the baker's boy on a bicycle, and set off the long way round the square, to put as much space as possible between herself and her tormenter.

'Miss Nicholls! Wait!'

That stopped her. How had he known her name? She looked around.

He was climbing down off the cart. Not the waggoner, as she had first thought, but a young man with fair hair who had been sitting up beside him. He came trotting after her, his brown overcoat flapping and his hat in his hand. 'It is you, isn't it?' He was smiling. 'Don't you know who 'tis?'

Of course she did, now she came to look. The boy from the front office at Bullivant's, the shipping agents down Penzance. What on earth was he doing here? She summoned a smile. 'Well, I'm blessed! So it is! Never expected to see you here, Mr Courtney! Whatever are you doing up London?'

It was the right question, obviously. Tom Courtney stuck out his chest like a pouter pigeon. He gestured towards the cart. 'Sent up special by Mr Bullivant,' he said. 'Valuable consignment, it is, for Mr Trevarnon – you know, up the big house.'

Of course she knew. It was a strange, painful pleasure, this sudden reminder of everything she had left behind. Tom Courtney of all people – from the very office where Denzil Vargo worked. But she wasn't going to think about Denzil. Or no more than she could help. It was like putting your tongue against a sore tooth, painful but irresistible.

Tom was still talking. 'We were going to ship the stuff down, but it's been in storage for weeks already with these dock strikes. And now these rail stoppages are threatened. Mr Trevarnon wanted someone to come and get it in person and take it home on the train, before it gets any worse – otherwise it'll never get there, he said.' He smirked. 'So here I am, large as life and twice as handsome.' He looked at her sideways, bursting with pride and obviously waiting for some response.

'My word,' she said, trying to sound more impressed than she felt. Funny, back in Penzance Tom Courtney had looked no end of a fellow, with his smart suit and waistcoat and the little feather in his hat. Denzil had been quite in awe of his style, she remembered. Here, though, he contrived to look quite ordinary. There was something old-fashioned about the cut of his trousers and his great thick country boots.

He said proudly, 'Return ticket, Trevarnon paid for. Up today, back on the night train. And the hire of a waggon from the station for me to cart it all with.'

Sprat frowned. 'But what are you doing *here?* In the square?'

'Brought a trunk up here at the same time. For...' he made a play of consulting a chit in his pocket, 'a Miss Raeburn.'

Sprat nodded. 'That's the old lady I work for.' As if he didn't know! From what Denzil had told her, she wouldn't put it past Tom Courtney to have engineered this trip on purpose. 'Top half of the house, number seventeen.'

'Yes. That's what it says here.' He pocketed the paper again. 'So this is where you are. Last time I saw you, you were working at some big house out at Penvarris Cove.'

It was none of his business, of course, but it was such a sudden relief to be talking to someone from home that she found herself saying, 'I was. Working for Mrs Meacham up at Fairviews. Miss Raeburn and her nephew were staying there, but he had a heart failure and was took bad. He'll be laid up for months. Miss Raeburn came back to London to sort out their affairs and brought me with her to help – just for a few weeks, while she shuts up her flat. Dare say that's why she wants that trunk.'

She didn't tell him the rest of it – that she had not so much come away to London as run away from the Cove, and from Denzil Vargo in particular. Denzil, whom she had loved, and who had loved her too – until his

14

drunken father had suddenly shown up, after years away in Canada, and spoiled all their dreams by blurting out the truth: the reason Sprat's ma and pa had disapproved of Denzil all those years. Not because he was an 'up-overer' from Penvarris village, and she was a Cover – though that would have been bad enough – but something much, much worse. So bad she couldn't even think about it. She pulled herself back to the present with an effort.

'...a pity, wouldn't it?' Tom Courtney was saying.

'What would?'

'If we had managed to miss each other today,' he supplied. 'I still remember that other occasion, you know. The ice-cream...'

'Yes.' She felt herself blush. That had been a dreadful afternoon. She had been crying like an idiot in the street – over Denzil, of course, before she knew what she knew now – until Tom came along with a big pocket handkerchief, a kindly word and an ice-cream cornet. She swallowed. 'And how is...' she was going to say 'Denzil', but her voice refused to cooperate, 'everyone?'

Tom made a little face. 'Oh, well enough.'

Sprat was suddenly aware of Megan, who had stopped polishing and was watching them with undisguised interest. 'Good. Well, nice to see you, Mr Courtney. Now, if you'll excuse me ...?' She would have moved away, but Tom came scurrying along beside her.

'Vargo is worming his way in, as usual. You know he's living at Bullivant's house these days? And getting to be thicker than thieves with Miss Olivia?'

Sprat nodded tightly. 'I heard.' She didn't slacken her pace. Drat the boy, couldn't he leave well alone? Though of course he would feel upset about that. He had been walking out with Olivia Bullivant himself, until Denzil came along. She tried to change the subject. 'And how's the office?' she said, without really wanting to know.

He put on his important face again. 'These dock strikes and railway stoppages are hitting us hard. And if the Great Western men come out too, like they're threatening to, the Lord alone knows what'll become of Bullivant's business.'

Sprat stopped walking then. 'Bullivant's! Won't only be Bullivant's, will it?' How short-sighted could you be? she thought – although she herself couldn't help worrying about what would happen to Denzil if he lost his job. But a strike would hit more than Bullivant's. There were people in London already panicking there wouldn't be petrol for the buses, or hay for the horses, or food for themselves, for that matter. Even Miss Raeburn had been laying stuff in! But she said, as if her words could make it true, 'Anyway, it won't come to an all-out strike, most likely. Mr Churchill will have the troops in and put a stop to it, like he did in Wales, that's what our milkman thinks. Lot of scaremongering, he says.'

'Does he though?' Tom said, puffing out his chest. 'He should have been on the station today then, when we arrived. Not a porter to be had, for love nor money. At Paddington too. And you know why? Because there was a big meeting in the station, that's why – hundreds of railway-men in uniform all waving banners and shouting, "Support the dockers." Had to carry the wretched trunk to the cart myself. Just as well it was empty. I only hope the trains are still running by the time I get back there with this delivery.'

'Well, you'd better see to it then,' Sprat said, suddenly weary of being reminded of Bullivant's and everything connected with it. 'That carter'll be tired of waiting.'

Tom gave her a knowing wink. 'Won't matter. Trevarnon's paying,' he said with a smile. 'But I suppose I'd best be off, like you say. Got to get this stuff picked up, and be back at the train before ten. See you in Penzance, perhaps. Always supposing that any trains at all are running by then.'

He hurried back towards the cart, and Sprat resumed her interrupted errand. As she turned out of the square she glanced back. She could see him directing operations from the doorstep, obviously trying to look important in front of Megan, while the carter struggled up the stairs with Miss Raeburn's trunk.

Drat! she thought, as she came to the main road. Imagine Tom Courtney turning up. Just when she had been doing so well at forgetting.

Though of course she had never really forgotten. How could anyone forget? To discover, after sixteen years – a lifetime! – that your ma and pa, whom you'd loved, trusted, quarrelled with, all your life, were not your ma and pa at all! That you were born out of wedlock, and that the glamorous, romantic aunt that you'd always secretly admired was actually your *mother*, who'd never wanted you.

Worse, it was Denzil Vargo's family who were to be held responsible for her mother's shame. Denzil's Uncle Billy, who had refused to marry the girl he'd ruined, though he'd been offered money to do it, and had run off to Canada instead. That was what drunken Stan Vargo had taunted her with, that day in the lane. Even now Sprat could hardly believe it. And yet it was true, all true. Ma had confirmed it.

And, of course, it might even be worse than that. Billy had apparently hinted that this was not his child at all, but Stan's own. So Denzil was not only an 'up-overer' from the village – which was bad enough in the eyes of the Cove – and a Vargo (which made him an enemy of her family) but he was at best her cousin, and at worst...

How could anyone forget a thing like that, even for a minute?

She was so frantic with her thoughts that she almost walked under a motor-bus, and then she turned right instead of left, and was generally so long getting home with the hatpins that even Miss Raeburn, who was a nice old lady as a rule, gave her a very sharp scolding indeed.

Tom caught the night train with a very good opinion of himself. His mission had been successful, though it had not been easy. He'd had to have quite an argument with a union official, for heaven's sake, and then go from pillar to post to get a specially signed chit to pick up the goods. But the fellow he'd finally spoken to was a Cornishman – he knew Bullivant's of old – and he'd been very helpful in the end: 'Any time, Mr Courtney. Just you ask for me,' and that had been that, though, after all the fuss, it had been something of a struggle to get back to Paddington on time.

But now Mr Trevarnon's delivery – three great boxes of it – was safely in the luggage van, and Tom had managed to hire a six-penny pillow, buy a twopenny pie and a cup of hot tea from the refreshment rooms, and even wangle himself a window-seat in the compartment again. He leaned back in his seat – 'third class upholstered' as the long-distance posters advertised – and looked about him.

It was going to be much less comfortable than the journey up, that was clear, despite the pillow and the 'upholstery'. It was dark for one thing, except for the lamps of the carriage, and every seat on the train was taken – perhaps because of the threat of strikes. There were ten people in his compartment now, crammed into a space that was meant for eight.

He tried to spread himself out a bit, but there was a hefty middle-aged woman on his left with a big wicker basket on her knee, too big to go in the luggage net though he'd pointedly offered to help her put it there. There was something very odoriferous in it, and the basket itself seemed to have hundreds of sharp ends, which kept bouncing against his legs and pricking him through his trousers. And it was no good stretching out: the man opposite was thin, but he had astonishingly long legs and big feet, which seemed to take up half the carriage, to say nothing of a snore which would have awakened Rip Van Winkle – if by any chance Rip Van Winkle had succeeded in going to sleep in such conditions.

Well, at least it would be something to tell them at home. There was a little milliner's apprentice, in a shop near Bullivant's – not the class of girl he cared for, but she had taken quite a fancy to him – and he imagined to himself all the colourful accounts he would give her of the day. Why, there had been a big black man and his family, all in colourful silks and carrying a big umbrella, walking down Paddington Station as if this was some exotic city on the outskirts of the empire instead of the capital of England.

Tom had never in his whole life seen a black man before, and he didn't suppose the little milliner had either, although there was supposed to be one who played an instrument in the Penzance Salvation Army band. She might have seen *him*, Tom supposed, although he himself had always taken pains to avoid running into the Salvationist band. He was expected to attend church on Sunday mornings with his parents, and that was more than enough religion.

In fact, Tom thought morosely, looking out of the window as the lighted suburbs of London flew by – gas lamps in every street, and even electric lights in some places – Sunday was not his favourite day. Mr Bullivant, the head of the firm, was a friend of his father's, and no doubt he meant well – regularly inviting Tom to tea in the parlour on Sunday afternoons, and encouraging a friendship with his dumpy daughter. Tom wouldn't have minded that (Olivia Bullivant, with her teeth and looped-up hair, reminded him of a rabbit, but she would be a very rich rabbit one of these days), but her conversation – whatever the topic under discussion – seemed more and more to revolve around the merits of that dratted Denzil Vargo. Tom was beginning to find her company very tedious indeed.

It was galling, that's what it was. Denzil blooming Vargo. Lord knows what women ever saw in him – great goody-goody lump of a miner's son, in his one good suit and hat, not especially handsome and too clever by half, though he'd never been to a grammar school like Tom. Yet there was Olivia fairly drooling over him, and as for that good-looking Nicholls girl, she'd actually been weeping in the street on his account! It was a crying waste, that's what it was. A crying waste! Tom laughed sourly at his own little joke. Mind, he had managed to impress her today – he was sure of that. She'd tried not to let on, of course, but she'd smiled at him, and seemed really glad to talk to him. That was one up on Denzil, anyway.

He shifted a little in his seat and got glowered at for his pains. He was beginning to wish he'd spent another sixpence and hired a second pillow, or at least a rug, upholstery or no upholstery. He could have got away with it: Trevarnon would never have noticed a few more pence on his bill. This whole trip must have cost him pounds and pounds as it was, just to get a few belongings down from London. Amazing what people would do when they had money. Tom himself had managed to earn a whole half a crown once, just by talking loftily about 'possible excess carriage' on a consignment. The customer had paid up like a lamb – though of course there was no such thing – and in the end Tom had been obliged to pocket the money to avoid complications at the office.

Tom smiled ruefully. He wished there were a few more 'complications' like that; he could do with an extra two and six occasionally.

Still, the money was nice while it lasted. He'd bought that penny cornet out of it, for the Nicholls girl. Pretty girl, that – he'd look out for her, when she got home. Supposing he ever got home himself. The train seemed to take for ever, and he'd have to turn up at Bullivant's in the morning, same as ever.

He closed his eyes, listening to the clacking of the wheels, and tried to doze. The woman with the basket got out at Exeter, and at last he was able to get some sleep.

'I see the morning train got in,' Mr Bullivant

said, the following day, as he and Denzil turned the corner of Market Jew Street and walked down towards the office. 'Let's hope young Courtney was on it.'

He wasn't expecting a reply. Denzil was walking a few respectful paces behind him as usual, carrying the briefcase. Just as well. Denzil would have found it hard to say anything polite about Tom Courtney – the blighter had never pulled his weight in the office, and Denzil was almost sure that once or twice he'd been downright dishonest. But there was no point in saying so to Bullivant. Old Mr Courtney was a family friend, and Mr B would never have believed a word against Tom.

He sighed, and trotted silently after his employer. It was quite like old times, except that these days Denzil rented a room in Mr Bullivant's house, and did not have to walk all the way from Penvarris for the privilege of carrying the briefcase to the office.

It *was* a privilege, too – a sign that a young man was 'training' and being 'groomed for higher things'. Denzil was glad to be doing it again, in fact: for weeks he hadn't been able to, because his face was in such a state that he wasn't fit to be seen in public.

It still gave him nightmares to think of that terrible fight with his father – drunk and belligerent as usual. Denzil had started out by trying to protect his mother and ended by laying his father out cold with the skillet. That had been the end of living at home in Penvarris – and it might have been the end of everything, if it hadn't been for Olivia Bullivant taking pity on him.

Poor Olivia (Miss Bullivant, he really ought to call her, but he'd started thinking of her as 'Olivia', by her own invitation) with her rabbit's-ear plaits, and her dumpy form dressed in sprigged muslin like a child half her age! She'd been very kind to him. She'd taken one look at Denzil's damaged face, and in ten minutes she'd talked her doting father not only into taking Denzil in as a lodger, but also into ferrying him to and from the office in a hansom cab to hide his bruises from the public gaze. Altogether, Denzil knew, he'd been much luckier than he deserved.

Much, much luckier! Because, of course, the Bullivants didn't know about the fight. It gave him guilty moments every day. He'd succumbed to a moment of weakness and told them he'd been kicked by a runaway horse – and he still hadn't plucked up the courage to tell them the truth. He shifted the briefcase from hand to hand, and glanced uneasily at Mr Bullivant's retreating back. Really, he would have to tell them soon. But it was getting harder rather than easier. Only yesterday, he'd heard Mrs Bullivant telling someone how brave he'd been, 'stopping a runaway', and Olivia was always going on about 'our hero' to anyone who would listen. Yes, certainly he must pluck up courage and confess the truth.

It was not going to be easy. The Bullivants were good to him: treated him like family, and invited him to dine with them often, instead of having his meals sent up to his room. A mixed blessing, that. When he'd had his meals sent up, he'd been able to put a bit aside once in a way – a slice of bread or a little bit of cheese, anything that would keep – and send it down to Mother on Thursdays, through the vicar at St Evan's where she went to scrub. Denzil paid her rent for her as well, although by the time he'd paid his own bed and board on top of that, and paid a shilling off his debt to the tallyman for his office clothes, he often didn't have a penny to spare. Still he managed, he comforted himself, and it was no good to give Mother money anyway: Father would only beat it out of her – and in that case you might as well hand it straight over to the landlord at the Cornish Arms and have done with it.

So eating downstairs had been a worry till Daisy, the housemaid – to whom he'd confided his problem – starting putting aside a few leftovers for him: little odds and scraps of meat even, and carrots that Cook would have thrown away because they were a bit wrinkled.

'Don't be so daft, m'lover,' Daisy had said when he tried to thank her. 'The Bullivants would be glad for 'ee to have un, if they knew. Only going out for scraps, any case. Only, I know how it is. My old dad had a hard time of it, afore he died.'

Only of course the Bullivants *didn't* know. He couldn't tell them, it was too shaming, and Daisy never would. But those bits and pieces made all the difference. He was happier now to dine downstairs (it also meant he had more to eat himself), although he made sure he was well out of the way on a Sunday, when that dratted Tom Courtney came. Calling to court Olivia, of course – with Mr Bullivant's blessing, too – though it was as clear as the nose on your face that Olivia didn't care for Tom any more than Denzil did.

Fathers, Denzil thought! Why couldn't his own father have stayed in Canada, where he belonged? Life had been so simple before that – living at home with Mother, walking out with Sprat Nicholls across the fields. All right, people had disapproved of that – her being from the Cove and him from Penvarris village – but they'd have managed, ridden it out, waited. And then his confounded father had come home, out of a job and short of sixpence for drink, and accosted Sprat in the lane – actually laying violent hands on her, it seemed, and threatening her with worse if she came near again! No wonder the poor girl had run off to London and wanted no more to do with the Vargos.

Still, it was no good dwelling on that. Here they were going up the office steps already, and there was Tom in the front office, already at the counter – red-eyed and bleary from going up to London and back within twenty-four hours, but still contriving to look immensely pleased with himself.

'Morning, Courtney,' Bullivant said, with an approving nod. 'You caught the train, I see. Manage all right with that consignment, did you?'

'Yes, sir,' Tom said, in his silkiest manner, which always made Denzil want to thump him. 'Don't you worry about that. I had a lot of trouble getting them to release it, but I talked them into it. I brought it down, and Trevarnon had a carriage at the station waiting. It will all be up at the house and unloaded by this time.'

'Good man,' Bullivant said heartily.

'And Miss Raeburn's trunk, too. Safely delivered, sir.' Tom flashed a triumphant glance at Denzil.

'Stout fellow,' Bullivant said. 'Good idea of yours, to take it up yourself. Two satisfied customers. Well done.' He went into his office and shut the door.

Claude Emms, the junior boy, scuttling in with fresh-mixed ink and blotting paper, gave Denzil a meaningful look and scuttled out again. 'Typical Courtney,' the look said.

It had been Denzil's idea, of course, to take the trunk. The whole plan had been Denzil's, in fact. Mr Trevarnon had come into the office fretting about his goods, and it had come to him in a flash of inspiration that Miss Raeburn also had a trunk waiting for shipping, which seemed unlikely to reach her otherwise. Someone could take up the trunk and come back with Trevarnon's goods. Of course he had assumed that, since it was a punishing journey, the 'someone' who went would be himself. To go to London, with a chance of seeing Sprat – he would have done more than sit in a train for sixteen hours to achieve that. Whoever would have expected Tom Courtney to volunteer instead?

Only, of course, Denzil had been fool enough to outline this to Claude, when he thought Tom wasn't listening. And next thing, there was Tom, proposing the whole event to Mr Bullivant, who naturally gave him all the credit for it. There wasn't much Tom wouldn't do to disoblige Denzil Vargo. Even when the trunk had arrived in the yard – on a farm cart – for forwarding, Tom had made a point of pocketing the ticket with Miss Raeburn's address on it, on purpose to make sure Denzil didn't see it.

'Saw your Miss Nicholls, up London,' Tom said now, with deliberate spite. 'Nice little talk we had.'

Denzil's fists clenched in his pockets, but he held his tongue. It was no business of his what Sprat did, or who she talked to, she had made that clear. He had tried to write to her before she left, but she hadn't even answered his letter. No doubt he had his father to thank for that, too. Well, he couldn't blame her. Though he would dearly have liked to go and see her, if only to talk about things. Of course, she might not have wanted to see him, but she would always be 'fond of him ... like a sister', she had said. Well, a man might see his sister, he supposed.

'Pretty girl, isn't she?' Tom went on. 'Some lovely smile, when she's pleased to see a fellow.'

Denzil could stand no more. He stumped into the back office, slammed the door, sat down at his desk and got grimly to work. His mood was not improved when, an hour later, Claude came in to say that Mr Bullivant was manning the front office himself for the time being. Mr Trevarnon had called in with a hefty tip for Tom, and such glowing praise for the company, that Mr B had given Tom the rest of the morning off, in consideration of his not having been to bed for the night.

Denzil said nothing, but he banged away at the typewriter fiercely, as if the letter on every key was a picture of Tom Courtney's face.

Two

Tom Courtney's visit seemed to please Miss Raeburn, who was delighted at getting her trunk delivered, when everything else seemed to be held up in these transport strikes, but it had been a torment to Sprat. It had reminded her too fiercely of the things she had left behind.

She remembered Aunt Gypsy (she still couldn't think of her as 'Mother'!) when she was alive, saying once that a man never appreciated his home until he'd travelled enough to have something to compare it with. It had fascinated Sprat at the time, and she had always wanted to go to places and see things. Well, now she had, and the more she saw of London, the more she missed the Cove.

Mind, it had been interesting. She and Megan had glimpsed the new King once, trotting past in a carriage, wearing a suit and hat for all the world like anyone else. Sprat had been rather disappointed – she had expected to see a crown, at least – but she'd joined in and waved with the best of them. Another day a woman had stopped her in the street, and Sprat hadn't understood a word she'd said until the woman whipped out a guidebook and pointed to it, and Sprat realised that she was foreign. Sprat knew about people speaking French and things, of course she did. There were always sailors down Penzance, and Breton onion sellers too, and some of the fishermen from the Cove could 'get by' with a word or two in France, come to that. But somehow Sprat had never supposed that there were ordinary people in the world who just went about talking another language all the time, with no proper English at all.

And naturally there were more shops and streets and people in London than she had ever imagined. More than she'd ever imagined existed in the whole world. That was the trouble with the place, partly. You could walk for half an hour in any direction and still be in London, with no sign of a tree or a cow anywhere. Lots of parks, Megan said, and the river – she and Sprat went there once or twice on their Wednesday afternoons off – but it wasn't the same thing at all. The weather was getting hotter and hotter, too. It seemed to beat back off the pavements at you, and sometimes Sprat fairly yearned to be sitting on the cliffs at Penvarris, looking down at the sea, with the cool grasses under her and a sea-breeze stirring the salt air.

And now even Megan seemed to have disappeared. Sprat had looked out for her for days, but there seemed to be no sign of her – not on the front steps or the staircase, or even in the 'area', beating rugs. Only the sour-faced housekeeper from downstairs, who glowered at Sprat when she had hung about hopefully one Wednesday afternoon, and told her to go somewhere else and stare.

So it was a relief, a week or so later, to come back from buying paraffin (some traipse-about she'd had finding it, too – all the shops were running short of things) and there was Megan, standing on the corner of the square with a big purple, green and white sash across her chest and a bagful of papers on her shoulder.

'Here!' Sprat said, going up to her at once. 'What you doing dressed up like that? And what are those papers? Haven't seen you for ages.'

Megan made a face. 'Lost my position for going to a women's meeting, isn't it? The mistress didn't like it, and that was the end of that. Out on my ear, straight away. Though it turned out all right. I've got a job now with one of the ladies from the Movement, look, and I can go to meetings whenever I like.'

Sprat gasped. 'You never are? Working for one of those Suffragette women?' This was

34

more exotic than foreigners in the street.

'Suffragists, it is,' Megan corrected. 'It's only the papers call us Suffragettes, look. Yes, I am. And why not? All sorts of people belong. Hundreds of us, there are, in London.'

'You're never throwing stones at windows, and chaining yourself to railings?' Sprat said, aghast. 'Kicking policemen and all that?'

Megan laughed. 'Not me. Selling papers, isn't it?' she said. 'Look, there you are. *Votes for Women*. Buy one, will you, Mina?' She held out a copy as she spoke.

Sprat looked at it doubtfully. 'Your new mistress know you're doing this, does she?'

Megan giggled. 'Of course she does. That was who sent me down here. Though Joe, the milk-boy, doesn't like it a bit. Do take a copy, Mina, there's a friend. I've got to get rid of all these today, somehow, and I'm not supposed to be on this square by rights. I only came down hoping to get a sight of you. I never had chance to speak to you before I left, and tell you where I'd gone.'

Sprat felt in her apron pocket for sixpence. For Megan's sake, she thought. And perhaps Miss Raeburn would like to see the paper. She'd surprised Sprat once by speaking up for the Suffragettes – 'suffragists', she should say! – and their movement.

'Now then! What's all this? You move

along, young woman, or I'll have you on a charge. On the pavement, too, instead of in the gutter – you know better than that. Obstruction, that is, so move along or we'll see how you like the inside of a cell.' A policeman had appeared from nowhere and was towering over them.

Sprat was astounded, but Megan was already packing up her papers and preparing to leave.

'Here,' Sprat said, 'she wasn't doing...' but Megan interrupted.

'Don't argue with him, Mina. You'll get me locked up, and I'm not sure I could stand being treated the way they are.'

Sprat hesitated, the paper still in her hand. 'But...'

'You too,' the policeman said, giving her a shove. 'Go on. Off out of it. Get back and mind your business where you belong. Votes for women, indeed. You'll be wanting to be in Parliament next. Well, what are you waiting for?'

Megan had already fled and Sprat, a little shaken, picked up the paraffin can and followed her example. It certainly wasn't the Cove round here. Back at home, the most you ever saw of a policeman was the local sergeant clipping some lad around the earhole for scrumping apples or swimming off the jetty in the altogether. A figure to watch for, perhaps, when you were small –

but as to pushing respectable women in the street! Sprat hurried home as if all the peelers in London were after her.

Miss Raeburn tutted when she told her, but said nothing more. She enjoyed the paper, though, and after that she started sending Sprat out on purpose to get it – though Sprat made sure she avoided policemen like the plague.

What would they make of that, back at the Cove?

James Raeburn, up at Fairviews House, hitched himself a little further up in bed and looked from his bedroom window down to the sea. If he propped himself on his pillows he could just see the cliff-path leading to the Cove, and the fishermen down on the seawall mending their nets. The sort of peaceful view he had come to Cornwall to find, although he would have swapped it cheerfully for a view of Belgravia. Just as he would have exchanged all the care and nursing in the world for an evening at his club and a decent brandy.

'Mr Raeburn! You are supposed to be resting!' That was the formidable Nurse Bloom, sweeping into the room like a typhoon and pushing her starched cuffs up on her substantial arms. Drat the woman. How had she known he was sitting up? She seemed to have eyes like awls, boring through two flights of stairs and a bedroom door.

'Yes, Nurse Bloom,' he said meekly, settling back.

'You stay there, if you want to come downstairs for an hour later on. We can't have you overdoing it. You've been very ill!'

'Yes,' James said wearily. He didn't want to overdo it, of course. He had learned that lesson the hard way. Perhaps he should have listened to his doctor's advice earlier – that heart seizure had frightened him thoroughly. There had been moments, those first few weeks, when he really thought he was not going to survive. But the doctor had found the doughty Nurse Bloom for him, and with her help and that of his man, Fitch, he was beginning to recover.

He watched her now, whisking around the bedroom like a whirlwind. 'You haven't eaten your digestive gruel!'

He took a few disgusting mouthfuls. Magnesia and bicarbonate of potash – what a thing to feed a man. But one couldn't argue with Nurse Bloom. She had the whole household running round at her command, and even his hostess, poor Violet Meacham, did what she said without demur.

In spite of the porridge, James smiled. He still thought of Mrs Meacham as 'little Violet', as she had been when she was young, although she was an enormous woman these days, and almost as much an invalid as he was – hardly able to stand up in case her legs failed her. But Nurse Bloom had taken her in hand. It had amused James on the two occasions when he had been 'allowed downstairs' for an hour in the afternoon.

'Now, now, Mrs Meacham. Doctor's orders,' Miss Bloom had bellowed cheerfully from the doorway, swooping down on the tea-tray and removing the chocolate cake from Violet's reach. 'A nice fish sandwich now, that's the ticket for you.' And Mrs Meacham swallowed the smoked salmon resentfully, looking at the delicate morsel as if she were eating worms. But she obeyed, however reluctantly, and had begun to do the deep breathing and arm-raising exercises which the doctor had been ordering for years. It seemed to James that she was looking noticeably brighter already.

Fitch put his head around the bedroom door.

James opened his mouth to speak, but he was too late.

'Mr Raeburn would like some more redcurrant cordial,' the nurse said, and Fitch disappeared to fetch it like a lamb. Yes, Miss Bloom was a force to be reckoned with. She had won Fitch's allegiance soon after she arrived, by defending him stoutly against Aunt Jane, who had stood at the foot of the bed and opined gravely that 'James is an ill man. He shouldn't be given whisky.'

Fitch had protested that if he was told to fetch something he was obliged to do it, and there might have been words, but Nurse Bloom settled the matter by saying decisively, 'With respect, Miss Raeburn, a glass of whisky at bedtime is positively recommended. Whisky is an excellent sedative.' James, in a haze of pain, had mentally blessed the woman.

He had changed his mind a moment later, though, when he heard her murmur to Fitch, 'I shall put a little potassium bromide in it, if the doctor agrees. The mixture is very calming for gentlemen.' It was humiliating, being discussed like that by the servants, but Fitch was clearly gratified by the confidence and had obeyed Nurse Bloom implicitly ever after.

'Your massage, Mr Raeburn,' she was saying now, rolling up her sleeves determinedly, and James was obliged lie back and submit to a pummelling. (When the doctor had first recommended the treatment, against dropsy of the legs, and promised to find a nurse to do it, James had been quite hopeful, dreaming of a gentle maiden with soft hands. He had been dismayed to find that the nurse in question was a strapping middle-aged woman with the strength of a bull.)

She finished at last, and had tucked him

fiercely back into bed – the covers tight as planks with their neat 'envelope corners' – before she allowed Fitch back in with the cordial and some letters on a tray.

James looked at the envelopes: a letter from Aunt Jane, in London, among them. He sucked in his breath. He had been afraid of this, ever since she went back to the city. She would have visited his flat by now, and he could guess what she was going to say.

He was right. 'My dear James, It has come to my attention...' Damn, damn, damn. How many unpaid bills had she found, he wondered? Lord alone knows what he owed his tailor, let alone his shirtmaker and his club. And the wine merchant, among others. Although, dammit, a man must live. And he'd hardly touched his allowance for a month – no doubt his bank manager would sub him a little.

But to think of Aunt Jane finding out! He'd rather hoped at one time that she could be persuaded to stump up for some of it. After all, he was her presumptive heir, and now that she regarded him as a hero – running up the hill, at his age, to save that Nicholls child when she was accosted in the lane – she might have been generous.

But now that she'd seen the extent of his debts ... 'It grieves me to tell you...' she had written. He looked at the sum she mentioned. Dear heaven! Did he owe as much as

41

that? Just to his bookmaker? Whatever would Aunt Jane think of that? He turned so white at the contemplation of it that Nurse Bloom thought better of letting him go downstairs, and kept him tucked up in bed with only thin soup for dinner.

Ma was getting seriously concerned. All right, Sprat had gone to London with Miss Raeburn in a tizzy, but that was only supposed to be for a week or two. They had only gone to get a few things together. Surely they should have been coming back by this time? And when Sprat did come home, Ma had something to say to her. She had rehearsed the scene in her mind a hundred times, waking and sleeping, and whatever Sprat's mood might be when she came – angry, sullen, horrified or grief-stricken – Ma was pretty well prepared for it.

Perhaps they should have told Sprat the truth earlier, but it was for her own sake really. And if it hadn't been for that damned Vargo, no one need ever have known. Sprat *was* Ma's child in every way but one. She'd raised her, worried for her, nursed her and ... yes, loved her, if you wanted to use that daft word. And Pa thought the world of her. Surely the girl could see that? And here she was, or rather wasn't, worrying them half to death. Ma wouldn't half give her a jawing when she came home.

But Sprat didn't come home. Not the next week, or the next. And there was no word of her either. Mrs Polmean from next door, whose cousin was cook up at Fairviews, hadn't been round calling in a long time, so there was no news there. Not that Ma was surprised: Mrs Polmean was still anxious, more than likely, because Ma's summer visitors, the Masons, had brought infectious fever to the house, and the doctor had put the place in 'quarrying-tine' or some such, and forbidden other people to come near them. But Mrs Mason and her daughter Elsie had been gone weeks – up to Mount Misery, where the fever hospital was – and Ma had rather expected Mrs Polmean to call. But there hadn't been hair nor hide of her.

Offended, perhaps? When Sprat first stormed out of the house, Ma had been that upset with Stan Vargo and his taunts that she'd shut herself up inside and refused to answer the door, even to her neighbour – who usually treated the Nicholls' house as her own.

Well, let her sulk. It couldn't have been helped at the time. Ma couldn't face visitors. If that story about Sprat's birth had got about, the Nicholls would never have held their heads up in the Cove again. But it seemed that Crowdie up at the farm had put a stop to the gossip before it started – Stan Vargo would have lost his bit of casual work up there, else – and Ma was beginning to feel able to face the world again.

A great deal she'd have given, though, to have Mrs Polmean drop over, on the excuse of borrowing a drop of sugar, and be able to say casually, 'Any news from Fairviews?', but there was no sign of that. Ma even thought of going next door herself, but she resisted the impulse. If Mrs Polmean *was* 'being funny', then Ma wasn't about to make the first move. Although she did wish now that she'd opened the door to Mrs Polmean in the first place – then she wouldn't have had to endure learning that Sprat had gone to London from talking to Norah Roberts, who always knew everybody's business before they did, and made sure everyone else in the Cove did too. But even Norah had no gossip from Fairviews these days.

Ma thought of finding an excuse to send Peter Polmean up there again, to see if there was any news. Peter was a bit wanting – what Norah called 'not azactly' – but he was a good boy and could take a simple message, and be proud of doing it for a few coppers. But she hadn't seen *him* for days, either. In the end there was nothing for it. She took her basket and shawl and, under the pretence of going up to Crowdie's for milk and butter, she set off to Fairviews herself.

She passed Pa on the way, working on the boat in the yard. They were planking now, and it was beginning to look like a boat. Pincher – as everyone in the Cove called Pa – was there, hammering happily away with Half-a-leg Roberts beside him. Ma half expected to see Peter Polmean there too, standing by with more trennel pegs, but there was no sign of him.

Ma was tempted to stop and tell Pincher where she was going, but she changed her mind. Better not. Half-a-leg might take the news back home to his wife, and if Norah Roberts once found out Ma's destination, you might just as well have shouted it from the housetops.

She nodded at the menfolk. 'Off up Crowdie's,' she called over the din. Pa saw her and ceased his hammering a moment to listen. 'Up to Crowdie's,' she said again. 'Get a drop of butter for tea.'

Pa nodded, and picked up his hammer again – 'Proper job!' – so she left them to it.

She had to go the long way, as if she was going up to the farm, and back down the road to reach the house – Norah's sharp eyes would have noticed, else. She would fetch the milk and butter on her way home. She thought about her dratted sister Gypsy as she trudged. Of course, one shouldn't speak ill of the dead, but that Gypsy would have tried the patience of a saint. Wouldn't be told, just like Sprat. Why walk out with a Vargo in the first place – a Vargo of all people, when she could have had anyone she liked? Half the men in Penvarris after her when she was young, and it wasn't just her looks. There was something about her – 'warmth and charmth', Pa always said – that drew people to her. And Gypsy too trusting to see. Just like Sprat, again.

The path was fringed by nettles; Ma hitched her shawl over her shoulder and cleared them back with her basket. It had been a hot summer, and the plants seemed more vicious than ever. The exertion was only for a moment, but the effect surprised her. The world turned grey before her eyes and she almost fell over. There was nothing to cling to, and she sat down in the middle of the path and put her head on her knees until the feeling passed.

She stood up, feeling shaken. What had got into her? She had felt sick, too, once or twice lately and yesterday she had almost wasted breakfast. She'd cooked some sprats that Pa brought in and then suddenly couldn't face them. She hadn't, surely, managed to catch that fever after all?

She put a hand to her forehead. It was warm. But it couldn't be that, could it? Doctor had said that infantile paralysis wasn't nearly so dangerous for older people, it was just that they could pass it on. And if there was any question of catching it, surely she'd have felt ill before this?

Get on with you, Ma told herself fiercely, most of the time you're perfectly all right. Worry, most like. That's all. No wonder either, with Sprat gone away like this. All for that dratted Stan Vargo and his poisonous tongue. She set off again to Fairviews.

The sight of the house almost daunted her. She was still feeling queer and the house looked forbidding somehow, all granite and four-square on the cliff, as if it was standing up to her as well as to wind and weather. But she went round to the back ('NO HAWKERS') and tapped on the door. She was preparing a face and a little speech for Mrs Polmean's cousin, when that wiry, grey-haired Florrie woman came out – Mrs Meacham's live-in help.

'Sprat?' Florrie said, when Ma blurted her request. 'Nicholls, you mean? She's not here. She's up in London attending Miss Raeburn...'

'I know that,' Ma interrupted crossly.

That was a mistake. Florrie was offended. 'Well then. That's where she is. And no, we don't know when she's coming back. Depend on the trains, won't it?' The door closed firmly in Ma's face.

That was all. Ma never quite knew how

she got back to the Cove. The ground seemed to be swimming beneath her feet and once or twice she had to sit down. She didn't remember the butter either, and there was no milk for tea.

Three

It was a Sunday afternoon again, and Denzil had shut himself up in his room, reading, while Tom Courtney held sway in the parlour.

He had never had much time for reading before – there were no books to speak of at home in Penvarris – and he was enjoying the opportunity. Strange old books, they were – Daisy, the housemaid, had found them in the box-room – all about missionaries, and thrift, and sinful people who came to nasty ends. Written for children, most of them (they'd belonged to Olivia when she was young), and Denzil, although he enjoyed them, felt a little ashamed of his pleasure.

Daisy, though, was terribly impressed. She could read a little, but it was a fearful chore to her. She came to his door from time to time, to watch him read, and marvel. 'Comes of being a clerk, I suppose. Seems some clever to me.' And when he had finished one book, she would fetch him another.

She was so frankly admiring that Denzil

might have felt uneasy about her intentions, if it were not for 'Bert', who seemed to crop up in Daisy's conversation with amazing regularity. Bert, it seemed, was coachman to Major William Selwood at one of the big houses nearby. He and Daisy had an 'understanding', though it had dawned on Denzil by now that most of the 'understanding' was that she would get married when she felt like it and not a moment before. 'Aren't fixing to start pushing a pram about just yet,' Daisy said. 'Need to do a bit of saving first, get a place of our own. Aren't going to do like Ma, and spend all my life in my mother-in-law's back bedroom. Never pleased herself once in all these years. We're young yet. Bert'll wait, if he wants me.' And it seemed that he did, because they'd been walking out for years. So there was no embarrassment with Daisy; she was just a cheerful friend.

Denzil was grateful for that. He seemed to have very few friends at present. Though there was Olivia, of course. Sprat had teased him once that Miss Bullivant seemed to have taken a shine to him, and sometimes Denzil wondered if it were true. But it couldn't be so, could it? Miner's son like him, and her the boss's daughter? But she did seem to wait for him more and more on the stairs, and she was forever finding excuses to come into the office these days –

and that couldn't be for Tom Courtney.

Only today, as Denzil was going up to his room, Olivia had come out of the parlour on purpose to say, 'Going up to your room again, are you, Denzil? I hope Daisy's found you some more books?'

Denzil smiled. Olivia was always so thoughtful. 'She has. Thank you.' He would have gone on up the stairs, but Miss Bullivant was still hovering.

'Only, if you run out, you know ... I have some others that I could lend you.'

'You are very kind.'

There was a pause. He put his hand on the stair-rail to go on, and Olivia said quickly, 'Tom Courtney will be coming to join us soon.'

'I know.' Wasn't that the reason he was trying to scuttle upstairs?

Silence. She turned as pink as her flounces and said diffidently, 'I wish Papa would invite *you* to join us sometimes. After all, you live here.'

Denzil smiled ruefully. 'I don't think so, Miss Bullivant. I should be in the way, I fear. Tom is a friend of your family's. Besides, I'm not on the most cordial terms with Mr Courtney. I shouldn't know what to say.'

She looked at her feet and said, in a voice that was almost too quiet to hear, 'Neither do I.'

There was an uncomfortable pause.

Denzil said brightly, 'Well, I should go. Your visitor will arrive any moment. Enjoy your tea party.'

She looked at him dolefully. 'Of course. Thank you.' He was almost at the turn of the stairs before she called up after him, 'And Denzil...?'

He looked down at her – bright-faced and earnest, gazing up at him. 'Yes?'

'Call me Olivia. Please. I thought that was agreed. After all, as I said before, you do live in the house.'

He found himself smiling. 'I will. Thank you ... Olivia.'

She coloured up worse than ever, nodded shyly and turned away. A moment later he heard Tom's knock on the door.

But back in his room Denzil found it difficult to concentrate on the mission to Peru. It was hard to believe, he thought to himself, but perhaps Sprat's observations had not been so unwarranted after all.

Sprat, in sweltering London, was wishing she was home. The city in July had been all cheerless drizzle, but the whole of August had come in blazing, and she had never known anything like it.

Like this afternoon, for instance. It was a cloudless, brilliant day: the sort of afternoon that, when she was young, she had often

52

spent lying full-length on the cliffs, smelling the scent of sea-pinks and watching the gulls swoop above the waves – or perhaps, if she was very daring, stripping off her boots and stockings to paddle in the cool waters of the Cove, until Ma came out and hollered at her for draggling her petticoats in the tide.

But here there were no sea-pinks and no tide, only the sun bouncing remorselessly off the houses and the stone pavements till the very air at your feet seemed to dazzle in a kind of haze, and even the tired plane trees and dusty grass in the square seemed parched and wilted with heat.

She opened the sash window, but that brought no relief. The still air hung heavy as a curtain, without the slightest whisper of a breeze to stir it. A dumpy housewife struggled by with a basket, her face damp and pink with heat. Otherwise the street was strangely silent. Too hot for people to be out walking today.

They would *have* to walk, too. The transport strike had London in its grip. No fuel for the motor-buses and no feed for the horses. Tom Courtney had been right, and Megan's milkman had been wrong. One after the other the railways had gone on strike, and now there was scarcely a train running in the country. Sitting here now, at the window, there was amazing quiet – instead of the usual rattle and clop of traffic, there was hardly a horse or waggon to be heard. Only the pigeons throbbed their bubbling sound, like so many feathered kettles on the hob.

Yet, if you did prick up your ears, there was a distant sound of shouting and crashing, and a shriek of police whistles – although whether that was strikers, or some protest procession by the Women's Movement, Sprat could not tell from here. Looters, perhaps – there was getting to be more and more of that, especially after a riot. Things were becoming so difficult to get.

Even supplies of coals and food were failing – no popping up to Crowdie's for a quart of milk here, or picking up driftwood for the fire, or digging your own carrots for your tea. Every bit of everything had to be ferried into town by somebody and carried home again from the shops. Without the docks, the carters and the trains, times were getting very hard in some households. The price of everything was going sky-high. Sprat herself had paid fourpence yesterday for a loaf of bread! Thank heaven Miss Raeburn had stocked up when she did.

My Lord, it was hot! Sprat picked up a paper lying on the table and used it to fan the heavy air. It was a copy of *Votes for Women*, she saw, with a notice for a nearby meeting marked in Miss Raeburn's careful purple ink. Oh dear. She'd regretted once or twice that she'd ever brought that paper home. Miss Raeburn had taken to going to these meetings – walking, of course with the present transport situation – and naturally that meant that Sprat had to go with her. An old lady like that could not be walking the streets alone at night, even if it was summertime and didn't get dark till late.

Boring meetings, Sprat thought them – full of endless speeches about politics and terrible tales of women being imprisoned and set upon by angry policemen with batons. She still found it hard to imagine, despite being shoved about in the square. Her idea of police action was seeing stout, good-natured, red-whiskered Sergeant Tonkins marching the likes of Stan Vargo firmly home by the collar for being drunk and disreputable in the street.

Still, at least those meetings passed the time. Sprat found it hanging on her hands, especially now that Megan wasn't there – and though she had looked for her at the meetings, Sprat hadn't seen her friend for weeks. And there wasn't even housework to do here. Folks in London, it seemed, sent out the laundry and bought in the food, and there was already a daily girl to clean the flat. Miss Raeburn's things had been packed up long ago and there was little, really, remaining to be done. Miss Raeburn was

out this afternoon with that lawyer of hers –
some fuss about Mr James's affairs – so here
was Sprat with her chores finished and
nothing to do for half the afternoon. Except
swelter.

She picked up the magazine again and
began to fan herself, feeling the hot trickle
of sweat beginning at her shoulders and
running, in a most unladylike manner,
down her back.

She tried to imagine the cheerful bustle of
the Cove: the men out with the pots; Ma on
her hands and knees scrubbing the step, or
shelling peas in the doorway with Mrs
Polmean; Norah down working at the nets,
straining her eyes and ears for any gossip,
with that ridiculous flower bobbing in her
hat.

She sighed. Perhaps she *should* have gone
to see Ma before she left. Not to apologise,
of course – what was there to apologise for?
– but to call in, that was all: see how they
were instead of just sending a message down
through Mrs Polmean. Wouldn't be so easy
now to go when she got home – the longer
you left these things, the harder it got.

Sprat looked out of the window. Apart
from a knife grinder at the corner, a fine
dust rising from his whirring wheel, the
square was as empty as ever. Miss Raeburn
wouldn't be home for half an hour at least.

Perhaps, if she wrote a letter – to Florrie,

say, and Cook? No good writing direct to Ma: she wasn't much good at ciphering, and Pa was worse, if anything. Besides ... Sprat didn't want to do that exactly. It would be like giving in. No, just a newsy note, sent to below-stairs at Fairviews, that was the ticket. They could get a message to Ma, easy as winking, just saying she was safe. Miss Raeburn could put it in with her next letter to Mrs Meacham. Supposing it ever got there at all, with this strike. The mail was badly affected, like everything else.

Once she had thought of it, the idea seemed obvious. When Miss Raeburn returned an hour later, Sprat was still sitting on the window-seat, licking her pencil, frowning with concentration and writing a long letter in her slow, laborious hand.

Tom's chance to make some money came sooner than he thought. He had overspent with Trevarnon's few bob, and he'd been looking out for a way to make up the difference ever since. He had been keeping an eye out vaguely in a number of directions, but when the opportunity came he did not even have to look for it. It was presented to him, as it were, over the counter.

It had been a hard week at the front desk, people coming in complaining half the day because consignments had been held up at some port or another, or were languishing in a railway depot up country. Meanwhile Denzil was tucked safely away in the back office, far from all the rumpus. Tom was beginning to feel resentful, but he had to keep a smile for the customers.

'Nothing Bullivant's can do,' he said for the twentieth time that morning. 'It's these dock strikes, you see. We've done our best, trying to find alternative transport, but it isn't easy. Half the country's doing the same and a free waggon's harder to find than gold dust.'

The customer sighed. 'Well, no doubt you've done your best. But I'm losing trade, no doubt about it, and this latest hold-up is the last straw. It was a special order for a wedding, and if I can't deliver it everyone'll hear. It won't do my reputation any good. Cost me no end in lost orders.'

Tom tutted sympathetically. The client was Mr White, from the drapery emporium, and he was more reasonable than most. Half the customers seemed to suppose that the delays were all the fault of Bullivant's in general, and of Tom Courtney in particular. 'I assure you, Mr White, the minute it is possible we'll get your parcels down here. Of course, we can't put them on transport if there's nothing running, but soon as there is ... You leave it to me. I'll make it my personal business.'

Tom meant nothing particular by that. He

said the same thing to lots of people, especially when – as now – they had a number of larger consignments already coming down by waggon, and a smaller parcel might easily be brought at the same time. In fact, of course, there was nothing he could do to ensure that – he didn't allocate the consignments – but it kept the customers happy, feeling that he was looking out for them. They were always warm to him in consequence, and that improved Tom in his own estimation.

Mr White, however, was instantly alert. He glanced around to make sure no one was listening, and leaned over the counter. He said, in a low voice, 'You do that, young fellow, and I'll make it worth your while. Strictly between ourselves, of course. Five shillings for you if it's here next Friday.'

'Done,' Tom said, before he had considered how. Then the enormity of the offer struck him, and he blurted, 'You sure?' Five shillings was a week's wages some places.

Mr White shook his head. 'Between ourselves, young Courtney, these strikes are hitting me hard. If I don't get this order here in time for the wedding, the dratted girl will say she doesn't want it, and what am I to do with three guineas' worth of swansdown and a crêpe de Chine two-piece? I can't return it, and no one else will take it at that price. Important customers, too. Daren't offend them, or I'll lose their custom – the mother, sisters and the grandmother too. No, I meant what I said. Cheap at the price, young man, cheap at the price.'

Tom was rather alarmed. General promises were one thing, but a particular deadline, that was something else again. He had no idea how the miracle was to be accomplished – he couldn't go up to fetch things again, even if there was a train – but Fortune must have been smiling on him. As he was leaving the office that night, he met one of the waggoners. There was a load to go up to Plymouth as well as one to come down, and the man had called in to the warehouse for it.

Tom sidled up to him. 'Here. You want to earn a couple of shillings on the side?'

The man was a big ragged fellow with a family to keep. These strikes were a godsend to him, though they kept him working all hours and all weathers. He looked at Tom suspiciously. 'Might be. Depends how. Aren't doing anything illegal, and that's flat.'

'Nothing illegal about it,' Tom said. 'It's a consignment, come to us in the normal way. Only it's been held up, like they are, and now there's a panic. Mr Bullivant wants it down here quick – carriage been paid and all that, you just indent for it same as ever. Only there's a new system, see, for special customers' – he was improvising wildly –

'I'll give you a chitty' (he still had that piece of paper signed by the union man), 'just like normal, except it might mean hunting for the parcel at the other end. But don't go saying anything, that's all. And return the chit to me. Special customers only, see? We don't want everyone knowing, or we shall have a riot.'

The man eyed him doubtfully. 'And the two bob?'

'Priority premium. Only we aren't putting it through the books, see. Don't want the world knowing.'

The man grinned. 'I see.' He pushed back his cap and scratched his head. 'Yes, I do see. Well, I might be interested, at that.' He leered at Tom suddenly. 'Only it'll cost you three shillings, young fellow. Take it or leave it.'

Tom tried to look affronted. 'Two shillings, I told you...'

'I know what you told me, my lad. And now I'm telling you. Three shillings, or I shall tell Mr Bullivant all about it.'

Tom thought of protesting his innocence, but abandoned the idea. 'Half a crown,' he said desperately, but it was no use. That offer was an admission of guilt and the man knew it. Three shillings it was.

It still left him a florin in his pocket, and Mr White was delighted. The waggoner was pleased, too, especially when one or two of

Mr White's friends began to call with similar requests. They had to be small items, of course, but in no time at all Tom had quite a little schedule lined up. Inevitably, he was occasionally offered a 'premium' for things that were already on their way. Then the money was his for nothing, though the waggoner still wanted his share. In fact, Tom began to feel quite aggrieved. He had the difficult job, of squaring the paperwork, yet he got the smallest cut. But he couldn't complain: someone would have talked to Mr Bullivant, and that would be the end of his employment – there or anywhere else.

Once you had started cheating the system, he found, it was very difficult to stop.

Four

'Well,' Mrs Pritchard said, 'fancy that! All them motor-buses and tramcars and being able to go on a train underground! And Miss Raeburn not even knowing her neighbours. Must be some funny people up London.'

They were sitting around the table in Fairviews, herself and Fitch and Florrie, listening to Sprat's letter. Fitch had been brought in on purpose to read it, since neither of the women was a great hand with 'ciphering' and it was generally felt that Nurse Bloom, although an educated person, was too much of an 'incomer' to be trusted with Sprat's news.

Fitch sniffed, and he and Florrie exchanged glances. Course, it was different for them, they'd both lived in London. No good them looking at her in that superior way.

'Well,' Cook said, 'go on then, read some more. I was only saying.'

Fitch cleared his throat in an important manner and adopted a special grave voice, like a parson at a funeral, which he seemed to reserve for reading: '... so hot you could fry an egg on the pavements, and people are paddling in the fountains...'

'Gets like that in London,' said Florrie, knowledgeably. 'When was that written?'

Fitch turned over the sheets of paper to look at the date. 'Monday afternoon,' he said. 'The day before the last of the Great Western railwaymen came out on strike. Lucky it got here at all. If she'd posted it the day after, there wouldn't have been a train in the blessed country to carry it.'

Mrs Pritchard, who felt excluded by all this city chit-chat, said sharply, 'Here, are you going to read that letter or aren't you? I got Madam's dinner to see to, I can't be standing here all day while you talk about London.'

Fitch exchanged another glance with Florrie, but he did go on reading. Sprat wrote a good letter, much of it about the bathroom: 'A proper china "throne" with blue roses all over it and a great gas geyser over the bath. You don't even have to carry the water or heat a kettle – it all comes out hot right where you want it. Mind you, that geyser's a spiteful thing – it's near had my eyebrows off already.'

'Of course, she's probably never seen modern plumbing before,' Florrie interrupted, in tones of lofty condescension, and Mrs Pritchard – who had been about to

64

declare that this was all Sprat's imagination – hastily thought better of it and held her tongue.

There was a great deal more in the same vein – how Miss Raeburn's house was in a square, and how it wasn't rightly a house at all but part of a house, and how there was a woman came into the square selling one of those suffragists' papers and Miss Raeburn had bought one and agreed to go to a meeting.

'I told you,' Mrs Pritchard said with a sniff. 'Proper queer goings-on, up London. Not the same as down here at all, if you ask me. Machines in the house for sucking up the dust? Whatever next! Never do the job like a good stiff brush! And meeting a foreign lady, too, in the street? Fancy! Whoever heard of such a thing?'

The others had no answer to this, and merely shushed her firmly while Fitch went back to the letter. 'She says, "PS, I would be very glad if someone would let them know at home that I am well." Funny! Wonder why she didn't write to them direct.'

Cook saw her chance. 'Because we aren't all London folk like you, with your all-fire cleverness and city ways. Daresay poor Mrs Nicholls isn't much for reading. My cousin down the Cove is just the same. Letter from London would only worry her.' She got to her feet, folding her hands grimly across her stout stomach. 'Now, if you've quite finished with my table, I've got that dinner to see to.'

'Nicholls's mother came up here,' Florrie said thoughtfully, 'a week or two ago. She seemed awfully anxious. And I don't believe Nicholls ever went down to say goodbye before she left. Is there a problem there, you think?'

'You London people would see problems in a glass of water,' Mrs Pritchard said fiercely, sprinkling flour on the marble slab to roll her pastry. 'There's been illness in that house, hasn't there? And the girl was told to stay away. Her mother is a friend of my cousin's. I'll go down there myself tomorrow and tell her. Now, mind your elbows out the way. I want to get this pie-crust rolled. Problems, indeed!'

But there were problems in the Row, more problems than anyone imagined.

Ma was feeling increasingly peculiar. So peculiar she hadn't felt up to going all the way to the top road to meet the meat waggon when it made its rounds, and she hadn't been up to the Penvarris shop for days. She had hoped to send up Peter Polmean – he was good as gold if you made him repeat exactly what you told him, and he'd bring back your shopping and your change as good as anyone else – but she hadn't seen him for an age.

It surprised Ma rather. He called by every day or two as a rule, and Peter liked to go up to Penvarris village – they knew him there and made a fuss of him. He was glad of earning a copper or two as well, so it would have suited everybody. Too busy down the yard with Pa, Ma thought, enjoying being a 'man' with the men. She'd ask Mrs Polmean to send him, the next time she dropped by. Supposing that she did call round; Ma still wasn't going to make the first move.

In the meantime Ma was making do. She was beginning to run out of things, and since that turn she'd had she didn't feel like struggling up the hill. Still Mrs Polmean did not arrive. It seemed that everyone was busy – even Norah was not much in evidence. Ma could scarcely remember three days together in the Row when someone hadn't come calling. Wasn't it just like it, she said to herself, when you are up to your armpits in soapsuds the whole Cove comes calling; soon as you want a bit of company, they're washing the blankets themselves.

She would never admit it to herself, but she was missing her friendships, so when the knock came on the door she hurried to open it. She smiled as she glimpsed a burly body on the step. Mrs Polmean at last.

But it wasn't Mrs Polmean, though it was very like her. A stout, grey-headed body in a long grey coat two sizes too tight, with work-reddened hands and a face that was slightly familiar. 'Mrs Nicholls?'

'Yes.' Ma was wary.

'You don't remember me? We have met once or twice. I'm Phyllis Pritchard, Phyllis Brown as was – Betty Polmean's cousin.'

'Ah, yes.' Ma remembered now. 'You're the one works up at Fairviews. Put in a good word for our Sprat.'

The woman nodded. 'That's right. And it is about your Sprat I'm here. Wrote to the house, she did, saying she was well and would someone call and let you know.'

'Ah,' Ma said again, not knowing how to handle this exactly. She stood back from the doorway. 'Come in a minute, won't you? Have a spot of tea.'

The woman shook her head. 'No. I came here with a message, and I've given it. I won't impose. Thought you'd like to hear, is all. Expect you miss her, now she's gone.'

Ma was about to agree that she did, when caution struck her. Sprat had probably told the woman to say that, Ma thought, in the hope of surprising her into saying something soppy. Just what Gypsy would have done. Well, then, Sprat had another think coming. She said, 'I'll manage. She'll be back soon enough, no doubt.'

'Not so soon as we expected. They can't get home until this strike has ended.' The woman leaned forward self-importantly. 'Even Mrs Meacham don't know when they're coming. Can't even find a way to send a letter, now, to ask them. Not without you find some carter to take it when he's making a delivery. And even the carters are going out on strike, so Fitch says. Mind, I don't know how he knows. We haven't had a London newspaper for days – that's been stopped with this railway strike as well.'

'Did—?' Ma began, but a voice from the roadway interrupted her.

'Phyllis! That you, Phyllis? What in the name of all that's gracious are you doing here?' Mrs Polmean at last, struggling out of her front door with her hands white from baking. 'And what are you doing calling over there?'

Ma gave her a smile and a wave, but Mrs Polmean ignored her. She stood at her own gate, and came not a step nearer.

The cousin said, 'I was going to come in and see you later, but I had a message for Mrs Nicholls. I've just given it to her.'

Mrs Polmean's face was white and set. 'Well, it is to be hoped that she hasn't given you anything in exchange, that's all. And as for calling over here, you can't.' The grim face creased and for a terrible moment Ma thought there would be tears. 'It's our boy Peter. Got that London fever, he has, burning like a furnace and can't seem to move his legs. As if he didn't have enough to bear, poor lamb.' She threw Ma a terrible glance. 'And we know where he got that from, don't we, Myrtle Nicholls? Sure as little eggs are eggs.'

'Here!' Ma started to protest. 'I never meant ... I mean ... Peter?' But it was too late. Mrs Polmean had already gone inside and slammed the door.

The woman who called herself Mrs Pritchard was looking flustered and embarrassed. 'Well,' she said, 'I'd best be off,' and she disappeared up the path as though the Bucca were after her.

'Wait!' Ma called, but it was too late. She glanced down the road. In every house, it seemed, the curtain twitched. Even Norah Roberts, who had found an opportunity to go out to her line with Half-a-leg's smalls, only nodded briskly and scuttled indoors.

Ma went back to the kitchen, and sat down heavily. Bad enough being sick herself, but this? Poor little Peter – had he really caught the fever? And the Row blamed her, you could see. She understood the message of those twitching curtains.

She'd have to get up to the shop herself then. No good asking the neighbours. And she'd have to be doubly careful – she didn't want to be spreading the sickness any further. She could have asked Pa, perhaps. But he had been in the house with Elsie

Mason just as much as she had, and anyway Pa was a man. Men didn't go shopping. She looked around her helplessly. She had never felt so bereft.

When Pa came home he found her close to tears, boiling a bit of fish because there wasn't butter to fry it. Haltingly, she told him all about it. 'First Sprat, and now this,' she said. 'It's like a curse on this household, that's what it is.'

'You mustn't blame yourself,' he said, mopping up his bit of fish with a crust of dry bread. 'You did everything you could.'

'Every mortal thing the doctor said,' Ma retorted bitterly. 'Jeyes Fluid, boiling everything. But you know what the Cove is like. They get an idea in their heads and they all turn against you. And I feel bad enough as it is ... Poor little Peter.' Peter was almost as tall as she was, but everyone was 'little' in the Cove when they were unfortunate.

Pa nodded. 'Norah was on at Half-a-leg about it – shouting to him that he should come home from the yard – but he wouldn't have it. If he was going to get the fever, he said, he had got it by now, and he wasn't about to let me down for a bit of women's gossip.' He sipped a little of his tea. 'So there's some as take our side. Not but what it's a terrible business for that boy.'

So Pa had known about it all the time. Ma was about to jaw him for not telling her

71

sooner, but he was in it just as much as she was. 'There's only a bit of jam tart for after,' she said crossly. 'I've been meaning to get up to Penvarris, but I haven't been feeling myself, with one thing and another.' Pa put out a sympathetic hand, but she drew away. She'd let him comfort her once, when Sprat first left, and she wasn't having that again. Wasn't decent, at their age. She said crossly, 'Never mind looking at me like that, Pincher Nicholls. I'll do. I'll get up there tomorrow, do a bit of shopping.'

And, though it felt as if her legs would fail her, that was exactly what she did.

Lunch-hour. Denzil closed up his typewriter, took up his coat and jammed his hat on his head. Just time to go down the Poldair estate office and see to Mother's rent. The vicar from St Evan would be in town too, like he always was on Thursday, and Denzil could send his bits of something back to Mother with him. He had his little parcel in his pocket. Nice bit of ripe cheese and a rind-end of bacon, and the slice of cold pie that Mrs Bullivant had given him for his lunch. Not very much, but Mother would be glad of it. It was a pity that he could only send home things like that – things that you could wrap up nice and dry, and keep for a day or two. Otherwise he could have done a lot more.

'Off out in the sunshine, are we?' Tom Courtney, in the front office, greeted him with a sneer. 'Boil half to death, you will, with that coat.'

Denzil ignored him. The overcoat pocket was the only way he could transport his parcel without being observed. If Tom Courtney had caught a sight of *that*, and knew what was in it, Denzil would never have heard the last of it. He went out of the office and down the steps, trying to put on the air of a man who might at any moment decide to put his overcoat on against the chill.

Tom was right, it was hot when you got out of the building. So hot that by the time he got down to the rent office and met the vicar (nice fellow – Denzil more than half suspected him of adding a little something to Daisy's odds and ends himself once or twice) the cheese in the package was visibly beginning to melt. There were greasy spots on the brown paper and it was giving off a strong, cheesy smell. The vicar didn't comment, but he wrapped it carefully in a piece of the newspaper he was carrying before he put it into his sulky-carriage with his own purchases.

'And how is Mother?' Denzil asked, as he always did.

'She's a wonder with her cleaning,' the vicar said. 'The candlesticks at St Evan have never been so bright.' He climbed on to the sulky and picked up the reins. 'I'll give her these when I see her. She says to tell you she is well. Appreciates what you try to do for her, you know. Appreciates it very much. So then, I'll see you next week, young Vargo.' He tapped the horse with the reins and it ambled off.

Denzil stood a moment watching it. So, Mother was well. Or said she was, at least. It occurred to him the vicar really hadn't answered his question on that score. He would have dearly loved to have gone to Penvarris and seen her for himself, but that would be to invite worse trouble – for Mother especially – if Father got to hear.

He sighed and started to walk slowly back towards Bullivant's. There was no hurry, since he hadn't taken time eating. He paused on the street outside the door, still thinking about Mother.

'You look troubled, Denzil,' said a quiet voice.

He whirled round.

Miss Bullivant, just getting down from a private carriage. She was going in to see her father, evidently.

He pulled himself together. 'Oh,' he said. 'Miss Bullivant ... Olivia, I should say! No, no. It's nothing. Just a little private business I had to do in town.'

She was smiling at him, a rather forced

smile, he thought. 'I saw you,' she said.

He said nothing. Saw him? What did she mean by that? Hadn't seen him when he handed over that bit of cheese and bacon, had she?

'Down at the rent office.' She hesitated. 'Not thinking of leaving us, are you, Denzil? Going away and finding a place of your own?'

It was his turn to smile. 'No, nothing like that. Paying my mother's rent, that's all. My father's recently come home from Canada, and he hasn't found work just yet. I'm tiding them over.'

'Tide' as in the Atlantic, he thought. Never likely to stop.

Olivia was looking at him, her eyes shining, the strained look gone. 'Oh, Denzil,' she said softly. 'I didn't realise you were doing that. You are *good*!'

She'd embarrassed him. He could feel his ears going pink, as they always did in a crisis. He said crisply, 'Nonsense. Always have sent a bit home. Anyone would do the same.' They walked up the steps together.

Denzil opened the front door – 'After you' – and, ignoring Tom Courtney's furious stare, went back to his desk.

He hung up his hat and coat behind the door, and set to work. As the warm afternoon drew on, however, he became aware of something unfortunate. From the pocket of his overcoat, hanging in the sun, there came the faint but unmistakable whiff of mature cheese.

Five

When he saw Olivia come in, Tom went to her at once, pushing past Denzil as he did so and excusing himself importantly from the customers at the desk. 'Pardon me a minute, there's Miss Bullivant come in,' he said, and hustled about to find the visitor a chair.

She thanked him, and sat on it. Nothing more.

Tom hovered a moment while Claude Emms went to tell her father she was there, but she sat composed and still, with her hands folded in her lap, and said nothing further. He felt rather foolish, and after a moment he went back to dealing with his clients with a poor grace.

'We're doing what we can,' he said again, more sharply than he might have done. 'There's a strike on. Haven't got a magic wand, have I?'

The man stumped off, and Tom turned to the next fellow. 'Can I...' the words died on his lips. This was one of his 'special service' customers.

The man, a big florid fellow with an iron-mongery business in the town, leaned over conspiratorially and winked. 'Mr White told me...' he began.

'So he may have,' Tom said frantically, signalling caution with his eyes. 'I can't look into it. Not just now. Perhaps, if you'd like to come back later?'

The fellow looked for a dreadful moment as if he were going to argue, but in the end he gave a disgruntled nod, and left. Tom breathed out. That had been a near one. He glanced covertly at Olivia, and was rather perversely irritated to find that he needn't have worried. She had been paying no attention to the conversation at all.

She wasn't even looking at him. She was smiling slightly, gazing into space or reading the notice on the wall – anything but glance in his direction. It was rather vexing. And he had his new cravat on, too.

He cleared his throat. 'Have you had a good day, Miss Bullivant?' If he struck up a conversation at least, he thought, it would be something.

She regarded him vaguely. 'Yes, thank you, Mr Courtney. Very pleasant. Thank you for your concern. But I know you are very busy. I must not detain you from your work.' And she looked away again.

He *was* vexed. That cravat was a silk one, and made him look rather dapper, Tom thought. It had cost him two shillings – he'd devoted one of his 'special payments' to it – and Olivia did not even give it a glance. Yet five minutes ago she had been gazing at Denzil Vargo, with his scruffy overcoat over his arm, as if he were the Shah of Persia. Tom was almost glad when Mr Bullivant came out and escorted his daughter home.

Well, he told himself, if Olivia paid no attention, he knew someone who would. He lingered deliberately when the office closed, until the little milliner came out to put up the shutters on the shop next door.

'Turned out a nice evening again,' he said, and watched her blush. 'Like me to walk you home, would you? We could go down the Promenade and have an ice-cream cone on the way, if you want.'

It was the first time he'd ever suggested that, and she smiled at him as if he'd offered jewels. Kept on smiling, too, all the way down the street and across the seafront. Quite flattering really. She listened to his stories, and even admired his new cravat when he showed her. Made a fellow feel a bit more confident in himself. And later, under the lamplight, when he offered to kiss her, she didn't pull away. On the contrary, she responded with such ardent enthusiasm that Tom, greatly daring, reached out a parting hand and gave her breast a squeeze.

To his surprise, she didn't seem to mind.

★ ★ ★

If you wanted bread in London these days, you had get up early. It was a question of going around the bakers to see which, if any, of them had managed to get hold of some flour. There were a few millers now bringing in their own, when they could, from the countryside around. Millers had families to feed as well, and grain did no good rotting in their stores.

She'd spoken to one fellow the other day, unloading his sacks, who said he'd come in miles and miles – from some little farming hamlet called Heath Row, right out in the country – and had to run the gauntlet of disgruntled strikers to do it. No wonder flour was hard to get. And when there *was* bread, there were always queues to buy it. So Sprat was very pleased with this morning's purchase.

She was turning back into Lypiatt Square when she saw the girl – thin, white-faced and wasted – standing at the corner of the steps. She looked so wretched and bedraggled that Sprat automatically put her hand into her pocket. She could spare a few ha'pennies. She and Miss Raebum managed well, but there were so many people in London who had been hit hard by the strikes – the dockers' and railwaymen's families worst of all, because there was no money coming in and some shopkeepers wouldn't give them credit for a penny.

'Mina?' The voice was so unexpected that it made her start.

But yes, it was her friend. Not that she would ever have recognised her. However had she got so pathetically thin? And there were great fading bruises on her face and throat.

'Megan? My dear life! Whatever happened? Been ill, have you?'

Megan shook her head. 'I ... No, it's all right.' Two big tears welled in her eyes and began to roll helplessly down her cheeks. Anything less like the old giggling Megan would be hard to find.

' 'Tisn't that new employer of yours, knocking you about?' Sprat demanded, with some wild idea of storming upstairs and enlisting Miss Raeburn's support for her friend. 'If it is, I'll...'

'No, no,' Megan said. 'It's ... I've been in prison, isn't it?'

'Prison?!' Sprat was aghast.

Megan nodded miserably. 'Threw a stone at a window, on one of the marches. I got three weeks in the cells. Second-division.'

Sprat had no idea what that meant, but she nodded understandingly. 'Heavens above! What did your mistress say?'

Megan gave the ghost of a smile. 'She got three months! In the next cell to me, she was. Educated lady like her, in among all the drunks and disorderlies, just like me, damp walls and a hard board to sleep on.' She sniffed. 'She was wonderful, Mina. A real brick. She stood up to them. But I couldn't do it. I tried.' She was half sobbing. 'I really tried. But after three days, when they came in with that awful tube again – and just forced it down...' She broke down. 'I couldn't bear it. They brought me some milk jelly ... and ... well, I ate it. I was so hungry.' She looked at Sprat hopelessly. 'I let them all down.'

Sprat was struggling to comprehend. 'You went on hunger strike? *You* did?'

'Only for three days,' Megan sobbed miserably. 'I wasn't brave enough. And of course, once I'd given in, it was all different then. Out of the cells and sewing knickers in the workroom. But I could still hear them, feeding the others.' She shook her head. 'I think that was worse. I shall never forget it, long as I live.'

Sprat looked at the pale face and the tell-tale bruises around the throat. 'Doesn't sound like you let them down to me.' But there was no comfort for Megan.

'I came to tell you, Mina,' Megan said. 'In case Joe's asking for me. I'm going home, look. Back to Wales. I can't bear it, staying here.'

'But how are you going to get there?' Sprat demanded. 'There's a transport strike on –

there's no trains or anything running.' She did not have the heart to tell Megan that Joe no longer called at the square. The milkman couldn't feed his horse, and there'd been no milk delivery for a week.

Megan shook her head stubbornly. 'I'll walk if I have to. I'm not staying here, that's the important thing. How can I? No job, no money and no home. And no vote either, after all we've done.'

Sprat looked at her sharply. There was a look of desperation about her friend. She did look half likely to set off on some damn-fool errand. 'You stay here,' she said, with sudden decision. 'I'll go up and talk to Miss Raeburn. She's keen on votes for women – maybe she'll help.'

She dashed up the stairs and told the old lady all about it.

Miss Raeburn was impressed. 'Well, bring her up,' she said, as Sprat had half hoped she would. 'One of our friends in the movement may be able to assist. She will be quite a heroine.'

'Thank you, Miss Raeburn, ma'am,' Sprat said with feeling, and galloped down the stairs again at top speed. But the square was already empty, and though she searched the streets for half an hour there was no sign of her friend.

She never saw or heard of Megan Williams again.

★ ★ ★

The transport strike affected Bullivant's badly. All over the country delayed consignments languished in sidings, food rotted in its crates and essential supplies stood rusting on docksides. Their own warehouse in Penzance stopped accepting goods for forwarding – it was already crammed to the doors.

Denzil did his best, typing conciliatory letters while Mr Bullivant tried to find alternative methods of moving goods. There were one or two private carters still running waggons, though even these were becoming fewer. The drivers had been stoned and jeered at by angry transport workers, and a lot of them had given up. Those few that did remain were having problems getting horse-feed. The price of their services got steeper and steeper, and the wait for them longer and longer.

Mr Bullivant came into the back office one day, looking drawn and tired. He put down a batch of letters on Denzil's desk.

'More of the same,' he said wearily. 'Can you see to it, Vargo? You know what to say by now. Anything out of the ordinary, bring it to me.'

Denzil nodded. 'Of course, Mr Bullivant.' Bullivant had long ago given up dictating individual replies. Denzil would type an apology, explain that the delay was due to the strikes, and promise to move the goods as soon as possible: Bullivant would sign it. Only with the most exceptional customers – those raising some other enquiry or threatening legal action – would Bullivant draft a different reply.

Denzil set to work. If only there was some polite way of copying the letter, instead of typing it out tediously time after time with only the names changed! But of course there was none. You couldn't use smudgy carbon for a job like this and they didn't have a modern stencil. There was nothing for it. He tapped monotonously away for hours. He got so good at typing the routine letters that he could do it with his eyes closed.

There were just three letters which needed a personal reply, he felt: a man who had livestock starving and two others who had been waiting months and were threatening to picket the office if nothing was done. He took them in to Mr Bullivant.

'Trouble is, sir,' he said, 'we need some kind of priority system. Some way of marking out the most necessary consignments and getting them shifted first. Everything's so random at the moment. You never know which port is going to start moving first, and when they do they just move goods from the outwards in, so things that've been there longest move the last. And people blame the company.'

Bullivant looked up from his papers wearily. He looked a defeated man. 'There won't be a company to blame if this goes on. We're making nothing, nothing! And there are still bills to meet and staff to pay, and carting is costing us double what we allowed for – even when we can find it. People are withdrawing their business in droves.'

'Don't know where they're taking it then,' Denzil said, moved to bluntness by his employer's despair. 'Every shipping company's facing the same problems. The docks aren't working. Neither are the trains. Waggons are being attacked. Nobody else can move goods, any more than we can.'

Bullivant smiled wryly. 'You tell 'em that, young Vargo.'

'Perhaps we could,' Denzil said. An idea had come to him. 'We could send out a circular, explaining. Won't make any difference, but people might feel better if they understood. At least they'd know we were doing our best.'

Bullivant looked at him. 'You might be right, young fellow. Might do some good. It shouldn't be too costly, and young Claude could deliver the circulars by hand. We could point out that our competitors are in the same condition. Yes, a good thought, young Vargo.' Denzil was about to bask in this unexpected praise when Bullivant added, 'I suppose you wouldn't care to draft something?'

That was a compliment and Denzil knew it. 'If you wish, Mr Bullivant.'

He took great pains over it, depicting Bullivant's as 'a fellow-victim of the strike', and asking for forbearance during 'this disruption to our mutual affairs'. It did read well, if he said so himself, and he was so pleased with it that he took the liberty of also drafting an outline for a 'priority scheme' which would attach red labels to the most necessary or perishable items in future, and ensure that they were dealt with first whenever possible.

Bullivant was delighted when he saw the documents. 'Capital, Vargo. Absolutely capital. We might adopt this priority scheme of yours. We may have to levy a slight surcharge, but I doubt people will mind. At least it seems as if we're doing something. I was beginning to lose heart, I don't mind telling you.' He amended the paper with his indelible pencil. 'Very well, type these up and we'll have them printed. When they come back, young Claude can start distributing them. I was beginning to think I'd have to turn him off – can't afford so many staff when things are getting so tight. But he can earn his keep with these circulars. To our most regular customers, you think?'

'With respect, Mr Bullivant, I'd suggest we

send one to everyone on our books. Other companies are struggling too, and a gesture from us ...?' He let the sentence hang in the air.

Bullivant looked at him narrowly. 'Very shrewd, my boy. Very shrewd. I have been underestimating you, I can see. My daughter has always said so, and I'm starting to think she's right. Very well. To anyone on our books, then. I'm sure I can leave it to you.' Denzil went out of the office floating on air.

If only Sprat were here to learn of this. Not that she would care. Or she would care only as a sister, he thought bitterly. And when, that evening, Olivia stopped him on the stairs, he took the opportunity of thanking her for her praise of him.

She seemed interested in his system and he spent far longer talking to her than was strictly proper – so much so that her mother came out of the drawing-room to see what was happening. Denzil was expecting a dressing down, but Mrs Bullivant simply glanced towards them, looked from one to the other, smiled and went away.

It gave Denzil furiously to think.

Six

James was getting better. Distinctly better. Now that he had stopped fearing that the least exertion would make him an immediate candidate for the undertaker, he was beginning to be increasingly irritated by his enforced confinement.

He was bored, that was what it was. Nothing to read – Violet's taste in fiction was for Aphra Behn, and he had gone through her dead husband's library long ago. It was not extensive: Rupert Meacham had never been much of a reading man. Not that James was either, in general, but a fellow had to do something. No newspapers. Not even any letters. That confounded transport strike might have been designed to irk him.

Violet did her best. His hostess had discovered he was fond of cards and invited him to join her in 'a hand' as soon as he was well enough to sit up long enough, propped up on cushions, in the drawing-room. He had positively brightened when she made the suggestion. But playing double-handed

Patience with Violet, while it was a break from staring at the walls, was not exactly the kind of card game he was accustomed to, and the entertainment quickly palled.

Perhaps it was as well there were no letters. Every time Aunt Jane had contrived to send word from London the epistle had been more severe in tone than the one before. He had been too ill, when she first went away, to take evasive action, and she had simply walked into his apartments and discovered the unhappy truth of his affairs.

'I have now discovered bills,' she had written the last time (and he could almost hear her scandalised tones as she penned the words), 'from your shirtmakers and shoemakers as well as those from your tailor. It seems that there are grave arrears in those cases as well and when I made enquiries at your bank it appears that there is not the money to meet them. I am sorry to write this to you when you are ill, but the more I learn of your affairs, James, the more seriously I am concerned. Incidentally, I was called upon by your wine merchant yesterday and I am more than a little displeased at what I discovered of your debts in that direction...'

James groaned inwardly at the recollection. Aunt Jane was clearly having second thoughts about that inheritance. Her sharp little note to him had hinted that she was 'consulting with her lawyer' – already – and at this stage she couldn't know a quarter of it! When she wrote she had obviously not yet discovered his account at the club. He wondered glumly whether she had done so now.

'Red queen on the black king, James,' Violet Meacham said, interrupting his thoughts. 'I win, I think. Would you care for another game? You are looking tired. Would you prefer to rest a little, and I'll read you out the letter I got from your Aunt Jane last week?'

He had opted for the lesser of the evils. At least, he thought as he listened, Aunt Jane had not trumpeted his concerns to his hostess. The letter was full of this silly suffragist nonsense. Aunt Jane had apparently struck up a friendship with 'a very charming and educated lady, whom I found most persuasive. It is quite appalling to think of such delightful women being imprisoned and shouted at, with no regard for their delicate feelings.'

'Delicate feelings!' James had snorted indignantly when Violet read the paragraph to him. 'Why don't these women stay home and mind their husbands? I am surprised at Aunt Jane. I cannot imagine my mother wanting to get involved in politics. And all these riots and smashing windows. Unfeminine, that is what it is. Well, if these people want to be men, they can be treated like men. Serve them right.'

'But men are not being force-fed, James dear,' Violet put in mildly. 'I think it is rather fine of Jane to support them. No, James,' as he began spluttering violently, 'you must not agitate yourself. It is bad for your heart. I dare say we disagree, but we will say no more about it. What news was in her letter to *you*? It was a long one, I see.'

And he had been obliged to mutter something non-committal to avoid reading his letter aloud and raising the subject of his debts.

But now there were not even letters. No contact with the outside world at all, except the occasional visit from the doctor. Only Major Selwood, whom he'd met once or twice on the cliffs, had sent round his card to enquire for his health. James began to toy with the idea of extending an invitation in that direction. Fitch was very good, of course, but he was only Fitch, and although one could chat a little to Violet and Nurse Bloom, a fellow needed masculine company once in while.

Yes, perhaps, when he was a little better, he would suggest it to Violet. Nothing fancy, just a little supper with drinks, and perhaps Selwood could bring his wife with him, as company for her. Violet was so much more able now, thanks to Nurse Bloom's attentions, that she might welcome a wider contact. Of course he could not rush it, it was years since she had entertained, but she *had* been induced to offer an invitation to himself and Aunt Jane, otherwise he would not be here now. Surely this could be managed, too, if he brought her round by degrees?

Once he had thought of it, the prospect cheered him greatly. Slowly and subtly, over endless games of double-handed Patience, he began to sow the seeds.

'Excellent idea of Mr Vargo's,' Bullivant said two weeks later, pausing at the front desk counter to speak to Tom. 'Sending out a printed apology. It's worked out very well. Glad I took your advice about him, young Courtney. Vargo has turned out to be good value. We shall see you on Sunday, as usual?'

Tom, who had spent the last fortnight wishing he had thought of the circular idea himself, could only grit his teeth and agree with as much grace as he could muster. He hadn't actually seen the circular, which irked him slightly, but it seemed to have done the trick – which irked him more. At least, he thought, Mr Good-Value Denzil had made life easier in the front office. The number of complaints had dwindled dramatically, and Tom no longer had to spend his day placating the irate.

Not until now, anyway. No sooner had Mr Bullivant gone into his office than the street door was slammed open and in stormed a man who – from his mottled face and the way he thumped his fist on the counter – was very irate indeed.

'Bullivant!' the man bellowed. 'I demand to see Bullivant.' Tom noted, with a certain degree of satisfaction, that he had a copy of the famous circular in his hand.

'Can I help you?' he said, in his best obsequious manner. 'What seems to be the trouble?'

'This!' the man said, slamming the papers on the desktop. 'Blooming cheek, that's what it is. Red labels! I never got no red labels. Where's Bullivant? I'll red-label him.'

Tom realised, with a jolt of the stomach, that he vaguely recognised the man. One of Mr White's friends from the Emporium, surely, for whom he had undertaken to 'speed' a small parcel from Plymouth. And here he was asking for Bullivant. This was not looking good.

Tom said, 'Now, now, sir, I'm sure we can sort this out. I'm sure there's been some mistake. Why don't you take a chair and we'll see what we can do.' He had learned long ago that it was harder to be angry sitting down.

The man seemed a little mollified. 'Well...' he said, perching himself on the proffered seat and adopting a gentler tone. 'It's these red labels, see.'

Tom was genuinely mystified. 'What red labels are these?'

It was a mistake. The man leapt to his feet, sending the chair spinning. 'I knew it! I knew it! It's immoral, that's what it is. I paid my priority premium, fair and square – and now here you are trying to charge me again for labels. I'll have the law on you. Where's Bullivant!' He thumped the counter, and shouted at the top of his voice, 'Bullivant! Where are you? I want a word with you!'

'Sssh!' Tom hurried towards him, flapping his hands in hushing gestures. The words 'priority premium' had given him a nasty sickening feeling in his stomach, and he said desperately, 'Now, now. No need to shout, I'm sure we can...' but the man shrugged him off.

'BU-LLI-VANT!'

The door of the owner's office opened, and Bullivant came out. Tom shut his eyes, swallowed hard, and opened them again. The world seemed to slow down like a goods train on an incline.

'What's all this?' his employer wanted to know.

Tom rushed forward. 'I can explain,' he gabbled, knowing he couldn't.

'*This* is the matter,' the customer said, shaking the circular fiercely. 'How d'you have the face to try to charge a man twice for the same service?'

'Twice?' Bullivant said blankly. The imaginary goods train slowed to a crawl.

Then suddenly it was all over. 'I paid my premium,' the man said. 'Mr White arranged it. This lad can tell you – got his signature to it. And now you want to charge me again. Well, I aren't having it, see.'

There was a long silence, and then Bullivant said, 'I think you'd better come into the office.' He showed the man in and shut the door after them.

Tom stood in the outer office, his ears singing and his heart thumping. It would come out now, there was no help for it. He seized a piece of paper, with some wild idea of resigning before he was dismissed, but Bullivant was too quick for him. The office door opened and Bullivant came out with the customer, who was looking subdued. They shook hands rather stiffly, and the man went out, mumbling and glaring at Tom.

Bullivant turned to Tom: a new Bullivant, icy and angry. 'In my office, young man. At once.'

The ten minutes that followed were too horrible to dwell on. At the end of them Tom found himself with his coat on and his hat in his hand, being propelled firmly towards the door.

'For your father's sake,' Bullivant was saying, 'I'll accept a resignation. Only for his sake. Understand that. You have twenty-four hours to write that letter and get out of my employ. Don't expect a reference from me, my boy, because you won't get one. Now leave, and don't let me ever find you here again. And I want a list of all the people from whom you have extorted bribes.'

Tom longed to retort that the red-label system amounted to the same thing, but he looked at Bullivant's face and said nothing. He wanted to ask for the wages owed him, but he dared not do that either. As he stood there, speechless, Denzil Vargo came into the front office with a pile of typing. Tom could have smashed his stupid face. Denzil was looking innocent, but he must have heard everything.

'Mr Courtney is leaving us, Denzil,' Mr Bullivant said crisply, making the snub worse by using Vargo's Christian name. 'Perhaps you could take over his desk in the meantime.'

Tom turned on his heel, furious. As he went out of the door he heard Bullivant say, 'By the by, Vargo, if you are not doing anything on Sunday afternoon, I wonder if you would care to come downstairs and join us for tea? Olivia would enjoy that, I know, and since Tom will not be with us...' Tom slammed the door. He had been meant to overhear. The final humiliation – Vargo crowing over his downfall.

Well, he wasn't beaten yet. He went straight to Mr White's and told him everything. There were a few angry exchanges, but Tom threatened to tell the town the whole story, and at the end of it he did have a new position – though it was only a menial shop job in the Emporium. And guess who had brought that about, with his clever red-label schemes?

One of these days, he'd get even with Denzil Vargo.

PART TWO

September – December 1911

One

Matters in the Cove had gone from bad to worse. Not Peter's health, mercifully: despite his mental weakness the doctor had pronounced him a 'tough little blighter' and he had come through the worst of the fever with only a slight limp in his leg and a weakness in his arm. He was still mighty feeble and shaken, but the outcome might have been a great deal worse.

The problem was the quarrel. Ma had made one attempt at peace, pocketing her pride when Peter was at his sickest, and going over to Mrs Polmean's with the offer of the Jeyes Fluid she had left over from Elsie Mason. It had cost her something to do it, too – her legs were still weak as reeds – but Mrs Polmean had come to the door with a face like a granite boulder and sent her away for her pains. Then, of course, when Mrs Polmean thought better of it and came around to Ma's, Ma had pretended not to hear the door and refused to open it.

After that, there was no going back. The

women in the Row ranged themselves, as they always did, behind one or other of the parties – though most of them took the side of Mrs Polmean, who had been 'let down' by those awful folk from London bringing sickness to the place. And that, of course, was all the fault of Ma. Mrs White, in particular – who had taken some visitors in once before and been guilty of cobwebs – was heard to remark quite loudly on the street that, 'Some people will do anything for sixpence, and never mind what trouble they bring others.' It made Ma mad to have to listen to her.

Pincher, of course, was peaceable, as Pincher always was. (The menfolk, in any case, were holding themselves aloof from the quarrel.) 'You should have let her in, Myrtle – never mind what she said. Poor woman's been beside herself, with that child sick. You two have been friends for half your life. And you know what the Good Book says about turning the other cheek.'

There was something in what he said, of course, and that made Ma madder still. If she had been feeling more like herself she would have made a point of going out and walking past Mrs Polmean's house with her head held high to show she didn't care and wasn't thinking about it in the least, but what with the quarrel with Sprat, and these funny turns she was having, she couldn't find the energy.

Norah, after a week or two of wary silence, obviously decided she could bear it no longer and – declaring that 'They two are bad as one another' – offered herself as a kind of go-between, shuttling between the rival kitchens bringing the latest bulletins of war. When Mrs Polmean declared to half the Row that 'Myrtle Nicholls would fall out with anyone – look at her sister, and that girl of hers,' it was Norah who brought the information. And when Ma retorted that 'Peter Polmean may be lacking in the head but he's got more sense than his mother,' she did so with the satisfaction of knowing that the mother in question would hear it before the day was out.

There was not, though, a lot of satisfaction in it. The daily grind of keeping up the house was taking more and more of Ma's decreasing strength, and every foray to the shop was a distressing struggle. Once or twice she considered asking Norah to help her, but the thought of her weakness reaching Mrs Polmean and being gloated over persuaded her against it. Besides, she did feel dreadful about Peter. Perhaps she really shouldn't have let the Masons stay. But what could you do, turn the sick girl out on the street?

Ma picked up her dishcloth with a sigh. There was no real pleasure in a quarrel when the person you were rowing with had been your dearest friend. And she was feeling peculiar again. She turned her attention to wiping the sinktop.

A little tap at the window attracted her attention: Norah, standing in the garden, grinning like a gargoyle. That meant that she had something significant to say. Only a really juicy piece of news would put that smile on her face. Ma wiped her wet hands on her pinny and went out to let her in.

'Well?' she demanded, without ceremony. Lately she had been embarrassingly grateful to see Norah and she was anxious that she did not let it show.

Norah walked in and sat down on the settle without being invited. 'You'll never guess,' she said, and folded her arms provocatively. Bursting with it, whatever it was, but not about to tell without a struggle.

Ma shook her head. Norah could be infuriating sometimes. 'What?'

'The strike is over. Winston Churchill sent in the troops to put down the rioting – mounted police, warships up the Mersey, and all sorts. So it's all over.'

Ma looked at her stonily. 'So?' she said.

'So,' Norah said. 'The trains are running. I've just this minute heard it. Mrs Polmean got it from her cousin. You know, the one who's the cook up at Fairviews. They've had a letter up there, saying that they'll be back before so long – Miss Raeburn and your Sprat.'

'Oh.' Ma found her legs shaking and she sat down heavily. Sprat coming home, and all this trouble in the Row. Absurdly, it felt like the last straw. She could not cope with any more trouble, she thought wildly, knowing she was close to tears.

'Here, Mrs Nicholls! You all right, are you? You've gone the colour of codfish.'

Ma took a grip on herself. 'It's nothing. Just this heat, I expect.'

Norah nodded. 'Could be, at that. Hottest turn of August for years, and it's gone on ever since. According to Mrs Polmean, there's been people dying of it up the country. So her cousin told her. It was all in a newspaper that came for Mr James.' She looked at Ma intently. 'You sure you are all right, now? Only I've got things to do...' She hesitated. 'I'll bring you by a drop of cake if you like. Save you baking if you're feeling the heat.'

Ma was on the point of saying sharply that she could manage, thank you, but she thought better of it. Norah had more tongue than a butcher's shop, but this was kindly meant. Neighbourly, almost. It might be the hottest summer for years, but it was not the heat that Ma was feeling most. It was the icy chill that had settled on the Row.

'Thank you, Norah,' she said, surprising

herself by how much she meant it. 'I would be glad of that, I really would.'

James had been planning his campaign with care. He had even permitted himself to be persuaded to abandon the games of Patience in favour of expressing an interest in Violet's albums. A time of life, he told himself, when she had been a social butterfly. A singer on the stage in London, with half the city at her feet, including of course his old friend Rupert Meacham. Memories of that could do no harm.

'Look at this,' he said one evening, indicating a particularly attractive picture of the youthful Meachams smiling over glasses of champagne. 'What a life you used to lead. Don't you ever feel that you're missing something, locked away like this?' He saw her movement of impatience, and he added hastily, 'Charming woman like you.' He had been going to say 'attractive', but honesty forbade it. Violet still had a pretty face, but – for all Nurse Bloom's attentions – the rest of her was still the size, and shape, of a haystack.

She rewarded him with a thin smile. 'You are incorrigible, James. Besides, I am not quite locked away. I have you here for company. And your aunt will be back soon – if she can tear herself away from those women's meetings of hers.'

'Of course.' James smiled. 'But even so, Aunt Jane and I will not be here for ever. I am starting to improve already, and shall have to go back to the city sometime. Will you not start to miss us, when we go?'

She had turned the page of the album and was looking at a photograph, tinted by hand, in which she was dressed up as a shepherdess: little red hat, a full red skirt held out with petticoats over a pair of charming little red boots, a laced black bodice and a ruffle of lace at the bosom which was at once demure and daringly revealing. No real shepherdess ever looked half so dashing, James thought. She had certainly been a deuced attractive woman.

She dragged her eyes away from the photograph. 'I'm sorry. What was that?'

James said it all again. 'I was thinking,' he added, 'while we were still with you – it might perhaps give you an opportunity? A chance to join the social circle locally?' He glanced from the album to her ample form. 'Now that you are so much more like yourself.'

'Oh, I don't know, James. I am too old for that, don't you think?'

'You? Never!' he flattered shamelessly. 'Look at Aunt Jane. She is much older than you are, and according to her letter she is all over London with her women's meetings and tea parties. She might appreciate a soirée too,' he added slyly. 'No doubt she will find it very quiet here, after the city.'

'Well,' Violet said vaguely, 'perhaps we'll think about it, when she comes home. Another six or seven weeks or so, she says. She's found a lot to do in London. Time enough to think about it then.' She picked up a fading photograph. 'Have you seen this one? Me as Iolanthe, taken at the D'Oyly Carte ...?' and they pored over the pictures once again.

James no longer minded. The first of the battles had been won.

Back in London, Sprat was counting the days. Of course it would not be easy, going back to Fairviews. All the problems she had left behind were still there, waiting. But she'd had some time to think, in Lypiatt Square, and she'd come to a sort of conclusion.

There was Denzil, for a start. The important thing was to avoid running into him. She had proved that she could manage to live without him – she didn't think about him now more than two or three times a day – and no doubt she could go on doing that, just as long as she didn't have to run into him every day. Well, he lived in Penzance now, and if he was courting Olivia Bullivant he wasn't likely to come bothering Sprat. She would just have to be careful to avoid him, that was all.

As for the scandal she had so much feared, that clearly hadn't happened. She'd had an answer from Fairviews to her letter – Fitch and Florrie had written it together. Not a long reply, but if there had been any scandal it would surely have reached them, if only through Mrs Polmean and her cousin. But there wasn't a breath of it. So Stan Vargo must have kept his wicked tongue quiet after all. Perhaps Farmer Crowdie had been right – nobody would believe anything Stan Vargo said when he had a bit of drink in him.

Of course, it didn't alter the truth – she was still Gypsy's bastard child, as she had always been – and it didn't excuse Ma, in particular, for keeping it from her. So, though she was going back to Fairviews, that didn't mean she was going home, necessarily. She might perhaps find an excuse to call down at the Row now and again – just to see how the neighbours were getting on. (Florrie said there had been more of this infantile paralysis down in the Cove, and poor Peter Polmean'd had it. There was one excuse to go down there, already.) She didn't have to call on Ma if she didn't want.

Though she couldn't stay up at Fairviews for ever. When Mr Raeburn had recovered – and Fitch said that he was well on the way to it now – he and his aunt would come back to London. Probably Mrs Meacham would want Sprat to stay on at the house, and in that case perhaps she would – Sprat was very fond of the old lady. But supposing she didn't? And Mrs Meacham herself couldn't last for ever. What then? She shouldn't go crawling back to Ma.

Well, there was a solution to that, too: those rings and bits of jewels that Aunt Gypsy had left in trust for Sprat, when she was twenty-one. Sprat had thought of writing to that awful Mr Tavy, the solicitor, and telling him that he could keep the money. She'd composed the dramatic words many times in her head: 'The price of shame. I refuse to accept a penny of it.'

Only she'd never written it of course. She was glad now that she hadn't. You could look at it another way – Gypsy owed her something for all the trouble she'd caused. That money would be enough for an apprenticeship. Hat-making, or something nice. She'd spoken about it to Miss Raeburn, who knew about these things, and there should be enough money, just about. If she was careful. And it came to her when she was twenty-one, so she wouldn't have to go cap in hand to Ma and Pa Nicholls to get it. So that was all right.

In the meantime, she longed to just be there – to look at the seagulls and the cliffs, and the wind on the water and all the old familiar things. No more pavements and trees and terrible hordes of people. It brought a lump to her throat to think of it. Only another twenty-seven days to go.

Two

The first thing she noticed was the wind. Sprat had forgotten how windy the Cove could be in November. As soon as she descended from the cab a roguish gust tugged at her new hat (a present from Miss Raeburn) and threatened to turn her skirts into sails. She needed both arms to reach the door with dignity, and she was glad of Fitch and Florrie (who seemed to be magically wind-proof) to help get down the baggage and assist Miss Raeburn indoors.

It was eerily quiet too, after London's crowded streets. The granite house seemed almost lonely on its clifftop. Even the garden dripped melancholy, with its bare branches and damp, fallen leaves.

Inside, though, a surprise awaited her. Fires were blazing in every room – no shortage of wood here, though the coal buckets were empty – and a cheerful smell of baking engulfed her. Florrie led the way proudly into the downstairs drawing-room, and there was Mrs Meacham, gigantic as ever, half sitting up on the *chaise-longue* while Mr

Raeburn (looking decidedly peaky) reclined on the sofa opposite. On the table between them was one of Mrs Meacham's albums, open.

'You see?' Miss Bloom boomed from the doorway, as though someone had asked her a question. 'A little occupation is good for the spirit.'

And indeed Mrs Meacham did seem to be fairly glowing with animation, although there was an eagerness in James Raeburn's greeting and in his questions about the trip that made Sprat wonder whether he had been enjoying the albums quite as much as his hostess.

Sprat helped Miss Raeburn in her room, with her washing water and clean underwear, and then helped her downstairs to an armchair. After that she was free to hurry to the kitchen and beg for all the gossip from Florrie and Cook – still united in a rearguard action against the indomitable Nurse Bloom.

'Fair turned the place upside-down, she has, since you've been gone,' Mrs Pritchard grumbled, spooning some hot fried mackerel on to a piece of bread and handing it to Sprat. 'Want a bit of turnip and a few licks to go with that, do you?'

'Licks' were leeks, of course, to anyone west of the Tamar, and the familiarity of it made Sprat's eyes prickle suddenly. She was home. 'What's she done then?' she asked, more to disguise her foolishness than anything.

'What haven't she done, more like!' Cook said, exchanging glances with Florrie, who nodded stoutly. 'Opening windows everywhere and laying down the law about diet. Not that Madam isn't looking better, and Mr James, too. But it's my kitchen, when all is said and done, and I can't be doing with strangers coming in and telling me how to run it. Tell her so, I shall, one of these days.' But when Nurse Bloom did come, Sprat noticed, Mrs Pritchard was as mild as a mouse.

Fitch came in next, for water for his master. 'Tore yourself away from London, then?' he said, and winked at Florrie. 'You'll see a difference here. Walking on their own, the pair of them, and the doctor is so pleased with them both that he's only visiting once a fortnight now. They're up there now talking of having a little evening before Christmas, and inviting in some people from the town.'

'Well,' Sprat said, pushing away her plate. 'That's a bit different, certainly. When I left, it was all Mrs Meacham could do to come down to dinner. But I'm glad to hear it.' She swallowed the last drops of hot sweet tea and got to her feet. 'Thank for you that, Mrs Pritchard. Fair set me up, that did. But now

114

I'd better go and see if Miss Raeburn wants me. She'll likely want me to unpack her things at once. If not...' She trailed off.

Perhaps, 'if not', she could go down to the Cove. No, not straight away, that would be giving in. Tomorrow, perhaps. This afternoon she would find a quiet job and take it to her room. The sleeper carriage on the train had been exciting, but not well named – the wheels had seemed to be turning all night, right underneath her ears.

But there was no quiet job today. Before Sprat had even left the kitchen there was a hammering at the door. Florrie answered it.

'Sprat?' she called. 'Woman at the door asking for you.'

Ma! Sprat thought, with anger and relief. She set her face into a stony scowl and went back to the door.

It wasn't Ma. It was Norah Roberts, with a tattered shawl thrown over her fish-stained pinny, and that ridiculous bobbing hat jammed on her head. 'Sprat? Am I some glad to see you, my lover. Heard you were home today. Just as well, my 'andsome, or you'd likely be too late. Better come down the Cove you had, quick as you can, if they'll let you.'

Sprat found herself staring. 'What is it? What's the matter?'

'It's your Ma, my lover, that's what it is. Took bad she was, days ago, and no better

115

now. Worse if anything. Your Pa's been beside hisself. Asking for you, she's been. I'm only glad I found you in time.'

'I'm coming,' Sprat said. 'Wait a minute while I let them know.' She ran upstairs and, without waiting to knock, burst into the drawing-room and blurted it out.

James Raeburn looked startled, but his aunt said at once, 'Of course you must go, my dear, if you are needed. I'm sure Violet would say the same.'

Mrs Meacham nodded. 'Of course. As long as you are back in time to serve at table.'

And Sprat, all quarrels forgiven, found herself hurrying down towards the Row. Thank heaven for Norah Roberts knowing all there was to know.

Ma was lying in her bed, drifting. She had been doing a lot of that, these last few days. Shaming, it was, lying here, with Pa leaving his work to run round after her and strangers downstairs taking over in her kitchen. There were those unwashed rags in the bucket under the sink, too. Lord knows what people would think.

She didn't know what to think herself. Fearful pains, there'd been, for days, and then this awful bleeding. She'd never known anything like it. She'd tried to carry on a bit, but Pa had come home and found her lying

116

on the kitchen floor and the kettle boiling dry, so she'd had to give up and take to her bed. And it was no good protesting, she near did the same thing again every time she raised her head from the pillows. And this awful floating, drifty feeling, where her mother and Mrs Polmean and Gypsy – and Sprat too – came and went in confused reality. Sometimes Ma wondered if she would ever get out of bed again.

Born in this bed, she'd been – her and Gypsy both – and now it looked as if she'd die in it. There were times, when she was tossed with that dreadful heat, when dying seemed a merciful retreat; but there were other times, like now, when she was quite calm and lucid. Pincher had wanted to call a doctor – 'Worry about paying him after,' he'd said – but the idea worried her so much that he'd let it go. Bad enough lying here tossing in misery without fretting about getting into debt and where your next meal was coming from.

In fact, she knew, there was no problem about that. People were good in the Cove when it came to a real catastrophe like this. Already there had been one or two sending in bits to tempt her appetite – though she couldn't eat a morsel of it. And what was to become of Pa? Only a pity she'd fallen out with Mrs Polmean – she would have seen to Pincher like her own. Even Norah Roberts had done her best – she'd got a recipe for 'strengthening gruel' from somebody who knew somebody who knew a nurse, and she'd made some up and brought it in.

Ma shifted restlessly on her pillow, and at once Norah seemed to appear, a greenish shifting shape, hovering above the wash-stand with a great bowl of something and saying, 'Found this up by the stile, surprised you haven't heard,' and ladling out strings of steaming fishing-nets which vanished in the air. Ma closed her eyes and drifted again.

When she opened them, the dream had not dispersed. Norah was still there, by the foot of the bed now, and this time Gypsy was with her, looking so like Sprat that the two faces seemed to merge, and there was first one and then the other in front of Ma's eyes.

'Ma?' the apparition said, and suddenly it *was* Sprat, kneeling on the floor beside the bed and taking her hand. 'Oh, Ma!' And there were real kisses, and real tears raining on her fingers.

Ma struggled to take it in, but it made no sense at all, only a great welling of relief and warmth. She said, 'Sprat!' happily, but it was too much for her and she closed her eyes again. She didn't let go of the hand.

Sprat didn't know how long she stayed there, holding Ma's thin, fevered hand and stroking the thin, drenched hair on the pillow. Ma had aged terribly in a few short months and, although she was burning hot, her face was as white as the bolster case she lay on. The work-worn fingers were as thin as bones, and her voice, too, had been a sorry ghost of itself.

A soft hand on her head made her look up at last. Norah, from some sense of delicacy, had stolen away, and it was Pa looking down at her, his face such a mixture of joy and grief that it tugged at her heart. She gently disentangled herself from Ma's hand and got to her feet.

'Pa!' She was so pleased to see him that she did what she had not done since a child – flung herself headlong into his arms. He did not protest, but drew her towards him and hugged her tightly as if his heart would burst.

'You've come, my lover,' he said, over and over. 'Oh, my lover, you've come 'ome.' At last he held her at arm's length and looked at her. 'I've missed 'ee something shameful,' he said, tears running unabashed down his stubbled face, and he hugged her again. 'Though I'm only sorry you've had to come home to this.'

Sprat, who knew that if it were not for 'this' she might not have come home at all, felt that a knife was turning in her heart. She was loved. What else mattered? She was loved, and she had half broken their hearts.

'Done her a treat, you have,' he whispered. 'She's sleeping like a child. We'll let her rest a bit. Come downstairs and have a drop of tea, and I'll tell you all about it.'

So Sprat sat at the kitchen table and listened, appalled, while Pa told her the tale – how Ma had been sick and off her food for weeks, and then complaining of pains in her back and feeling faint as a feather. 'Gone clumsy, she was,' Pa said, 'like as if her hands didn't belong to her, and then one day I came and found her – stretching her length on the floor with a bucket of water beside her, bleeding like a pig. I wanted to fetch a doctor then, but she wouldn't have it. Shouldn't have said nothing, that's what – but it only makes her worse, fretting where we would find the money. I can't do much fishing with her like this, and there's nothing coming in.'

Sprat wanted to say something comforting, but did not know how. She got up to swill the teapot and fetch the little buns that one of the neighbours had brought in. 'Cove folk are good, anyroad,' she said.

Pa heaved a great sigh. 'That's the worst of it, my lover. Fell out with Mrs Polmean, she did, back in the summer, and it's been worse than purgatory round here ever since. All over a bit of nothing, seems to me. Their Peter got the fever, and they blamed Ma –

too upset to think straight if you ask me –
and then, when they wanted to forgive, she
wouldn't have it. You know what your Ma is
like – stubborn as a whelk. Sets her mind on
something and nothing'll shift her.'

Sprat did know. She had been guilty of
much the same herself.

'Mrs Polmean is out there now,' Pa went
on miserably. 'Been hanging round the gate
for half the morning, but she hasn't spoken
and I haven't liked to say anything. Miserable, it is.'

Sprat glanced through the window. She
could see Mrs Polmean now, hovering by
the sea-wall, pretending to be picking up
driftwood for the fire. Dying for a word,
Sprat guessed, and she found an excuse
to go out to the water-butt for the kettle.
'Afternoon, Mrs Polmean,' she said, loudly
enough for all the Row to hear. 'Lovely to
see you again. Though it's some sad to come
home and find Ma in this state.'

There was the fraction of a hesitation, and
then the woman nodded faintly. 'Afternoon!' She gathered up her sticks in her
pinny and disappeared in the direction of
her home.

No use, Sprat thought despondently, but
she was wrong. Even before she'd filled the
ewer Mrs Polmean was back, carrying a
plate of splits and making frantic signals
with her eyes. Sprat went over to the gate.

'Didn't want to butt in, my 'andsome,' Mrs Polmean said, leaning forward so as not to be overheard, 'and 'tisn't my place to say anything, things being what they are. Only...' She trailed off, and glanced nervously at the house. 'Only, it *is* your Ma, and we were friends for years...'

'Course you have been,' Sprat said. She took the bull by the horns. 'We were some sorry to hear your Peter had been ill.'

'He's a lot better now,' Mrs Polmean said. 'And course, it wasn't your Ma's fault, when you come to think. She never knew the girl had fever when she came. You tell her that, from me?'

'I will, of course,' Sprat said. 'That dratted fever! I just hope she hasn't picked it up herself. Pretty poorly in there, she is.'

'So Norah told me,' Mrs Polmean said. She was looking drawn and miserable. 'Thing is, it doesn't sound like the same fever, from what I hear ... Course, I couldn't say anything to Pincher, and I could be wrong, but – well...'

'Go on.'

'Them rags she had soaking in the kitchen. From what Norah says, well ... If it was me, I'd have thought I'd fallen ... you know ... in that way.'

'Fallen?' For a moment Sprat didn't understand and then she said, disbelievingly, 'A baby? Surely not.'

'Isn't likely, I suppose, at her age. But all that pain and bleeding? Sounds awful like it to me, as if she had a dead child and it hasn't come away proper. Hope it isn't, Sprat – could kill her, if it was. If I was your Pa I'd get a doctor to her quick smart, and never mind what she says. Only it's no good me saying anything, he wouldn't listen to me.'

Sprat's mind was working overtime. Mrs Polmean had been famous in the Cove at one time for helping women have babies. If anyone would know, she would.

'You think that's what it is?'

Mrs Polmean shrugged. 'Looks like it to me. Course I haven't seen her for a long time. She'd know the signs you'd think. And 'tisn't as if it was her first – you'd think she would have guessed. But I don't know. You ask your Pa. I don't know if he's thought of it.'

Sprat thought of Pa's face, full of bafflement and grief. 'I'm sure he hasn't.' But if there had been a baby, she thought, it *was* the first time for Ma. Only of course Mrs Polmean didn't know that. Perhaps Ma hadn't recognised the signs. She said aloud, 'Perhaps Ma didn't know either.'

Mrs Polmean looked pitying. 'Must have done. 'Tisn't something you forget. Though I suppose it's a long time since you were born. No, probably I'm wrong. Could be something else altogether – but she wants a doctor, Sprat, that's what I'm saying. Time enough to worry about money afterwards.'

Sprat thought for a moment, and then she had an idea so stunning in its simplicity that she exclaimed aloud. 'Gypsy! Of course!'

She turned to Mrs Polmean, who was staring at her in astonishment. 'I've got money, or at least money coming. I'll have a doctor to her, straight off, this very afternoon. Here, you go on getting the water and I'll go in and speak to Pa.'

Mrs Polmean looked at the jug doubtfully. 'You sure? I brought these few splits for you, but she might not want me...'

'Course she will,' Sprat called over her shoulder. She took the splits and went in to tell Pa.

He was pleased with the splits – you could see it in his eyes – but when she mentioned her idea about the money, he seemed reluctant.

'I've thought of that a hundred times, Sprat, tell you the truth. But we couldn't take it. You know how it was. In trust for you, it is. Got to account to Tavy for every penny. I can't go using it for other things.'

Sprat took him by the shoulders and gave him a little shake. 'This isn't other things. This *is* for me! We'll send for a doctor right away, and I'll call by and see Tavy tomorrow. Come on, say yes. It needs you, you'll have to sign something. What better use for it could there be? Ma is more of a parent to me than Gypsy ever was. And you too, you stubborn, ridiculous man.'

He shook his head. People in the Cove didn't like having doctors, it was like admitting that someone was likely to die. 'But...'

'No buts. You just say yes.' She was desperate. Mrs Polmean would be coming in with the kettle and water jug.

He didn't say yes. Instead he said, 'There's more than fourteen pound of it upstairs, this very minute. Ma got it for that ring that Gypsy gave her – she told Ma to sell it for you, just before she died. Fifteen guineas she got. Used a pound to kit you out with new boots in the spring, but I've got the rest of it in a sock under the mattress. Couldn't touch it, I thought, because I'd have Tavy to answer to, and I couldn't get any kind of word to you to ask you about it. Ma was starting to believe you were never coming back – though I always said you would. Anyhow, the money was ... a bit of you, like, still in the house.'

'Daft thing!' Sprat said, but there was a lump in her throat. 'Well, I'm here now. You send for that doctor.' She looked at Pa. 'I shouldn't have gone away like that, without saying. I love you, the pair of you. And why wouldn't I? You're my mother and father, and no one ever had better.' She gave him an affectionate punch to cover her embarrassment. There were tears in his eyes, and it didn't do to see a grown man cry. 'I'm off, I'll just slip upstairs and say goodbye to Ma.'

Ma was half asleep but she opened one eye. 'I'm going now,' Sprat whispered. 'But I'll be back tomorrow. Pa's all right. Mrs Polmean's downstairs. Come to see what she can do and says to tell you she is sorry if she spoke out of turn.'

She looked at Ma anxiously and was relieved to see a ghost of the old triumphant smile light the fevered face. 'So she's seen sense at last, has she? Spoke out of turn – I should say she did. Still, I dare say I might have said the same thing in her place. Perhaps I *should* have turned the other cheek, like Pincher said. Well, if she's here, she's here, and maybe it's as well for your Pa's sake. Make sure she doesn't...' But the voice was fading and Ma had drifted again.

It was all the peace offering anyone was going to get. Sprat squeezed her fingers. 'I'll look in tomorrow – just see you have good news for me, that's all.' She went downstairs.

Mrs Polmean was already in the kitchen, setting the kettle on the hearth. Sprat gave her a quick approving nod, and the woman said briskly, 'Well now, Pincher Nicholls, what are we going to get for your tea?'

It was a much happier Sprat who went back up the hill.

Three

James Raeburn was, if not exactly on his feet again, at least very nearly so, and the idea of this little supper party before Christmas was being actively discussed. Even Nurse Bloom had not forbidden it, though she had so many strictures on food and drink and on how quiet it must be that James sometimes wondered whether anyone would want to come at all. Even supposing that Violet made up her mind to do it.

Then Selwood himself unwittingly strengthened his hand, by dropping James an invitation to a Boxing Day shoot on his estate. James had never lifted a gun in his life, but his illness gave him an elegant excuse to decline while at the same time affording a perfect opportunity to return the offer of hospitality. Of course, there was no guarantee that the major and his lady would accept, but Aunt Jane added her voice to the persuasion and at last Violet agreed, sending off a letter in her spiky hand and, once that was done, suddenly becoming quite animated by the idea.

She took to spending hours with her wardrobe and – under Nurse Bloom's approving eye – taking a few waddling steps into the garden. James, too, was being permitted ten-minute walks 'in the air' when the weather was dry and – now that there was some prospect of entertainment here – there was even hope of his being able to return to London by Easter (to Fitch's undisguised delight). Altogether things were looking up.

He was still concerned about his standing with Aunt Jane. She had returned from London with a very disapproving air, and was still inclined to draw her breath in sharply and frown whenever any kind of spending was mentioned. He had been quite worried for his inheritance, but fortunately the old lady had developed other interests. She was still in correspondence with one of her new acquaintances in London – some other old lady, James supposed, who was vaguely sympathetic to those suffragists.

He was indulgently amused. No doubt it gave the old lady a clandestine thrill to know people on the edges of the movement and write scandalised letters to her friend about it, just as Violet loved to tell you that one of her music-hall acquaintances had done something deliciously outrageous and got into the papers. At least, he thought, it gave her something else to think about beyond his deplorable financial dealings with his tailor.

He had come down one Saturday morning after breakfast, more or less unaided, and was looking in a desultory fashion at the letters waiting on the tray. Too early for a reply from Selwood, although he was still hopeful that curiosity, if nothing else, would tempt the major to accept.

There was very little for him, only a bill from his shirtmaker (again!). He picked it up quickly, before his aunt should see it, and as he did so his attention was caught by a fat envelope addressed – in bold purple ink and a firm, flowing hand – to Aunt Jane herself. He turned it over idly and saw the address of the sender on the back. 'From Mrs Pethick Lawrence, 4 Clement's Inn.'

He was still staring at the envelope when his aunt came into the hall.

'Good-morning, James.' She glanced at his face. 'Is something the matter?'

She was so self-possessed, so prim and Aunt-Jane-like, that he was the more incensed. He found himself saying, in an outraged tone, 'Is this *yours*?'

She took the envelope he had thrust at her. 'It seems so, James, from the inscription.'

'And do you know from whom it is come?' He was blustering now.

'Yes, dear, it is from Emmeline Pethick

Lawrence. As you have obviously seen for yourself.'

'At Clement's Inn?'

'At Clement's Inn.'

Her coolness infuriated him. 'And you know what Four, Clement's Inn is? This is no little-old-lady sympathiser. That is the address of the headquarters of this whole damned Women's Movement. I've seen it in the papers.'

'Yes, dear, I know,' she said mildly. 'It operates from a spare room in the Pethick Lawrences' flat. Emmeline and her husband publish the suffragist paper there.'

For a moment he was so angry that he could not speak. Then he managed, 'And this woman writes to you?'

'Yes, James. As you see. And don't speak of her like that. She's a very nice woman.' She was opening the letter, actually opening it in front of his eyes, in defiance of his clearest wishes. He snatched it from her.

'Well, I won't have it, do you hear? I forbid you, absolutely, to have anything to do with these...' words failed him, '... these misfits. Did you see the paper yesterday? Look, look at this...' He seized the copy of *The Times* from the table and waved it in front of her. '... Window-smashing Shocks West End. That's your famous Mrs Lawrence for you.'

'James!' She was formidable when roused, despite the slightness of her form. 'You will give me my letter at once. Or shall I call the servants? That is my property.'

He handed it over, sheepishly.

'And as for forbidding me to correspond with my friend, I think you over-estimate your authority. You are not my father, you are not my brother – you are not even my son. I am an independent woman, James, and I shall do as I please. And it pleases me to write to Mrs Lawrence.'

He was amazed at her resolve, but he was rattled, too. 'I suppose this is the woman you mentioned when you wrote. The one with the "delicate feelings" you were so concerned for?'

'Of course.'

She was so calm that she infuriated him. He muttered sullenly, 'Delicate feelings? That law breaker?' His aunt was supposed to be deaf, but her hearing suddenly seemed miraculously sharp.

'Yes, James,' she said, 'that law breaker.' She walked to the hall-stand and rang the bell.

The young maidservant came running in.

Aunt Jane fixed him with a look, and said to the girl, 'Nicholls, I shall want you to go up later with a letter. It is important that it catches the post today.' She paused, looking at him again. 'And on Monday, I should like you to go into Penzance for me and deliver another message, in person. I intend to join the Women's Social and Political Union and I shall also send a donation. I should have done this long ago. You may find me in the morning room in an hour. That will be all.' She swept out, taking her letter with her.

James watched her go. That speech may have been delivered to Nicholls but it had been intended for him. Every word. Drat Aunt Jane. He was breathing heavily and he could feel his heart pounding. This kind of excitement was not good for him. Didn't people understand that he was ill?

He felt his way to a chair and sat down unsteadily. It was some minutes before he felt well enough to ring the bell and summon Fitch to help him back to bed.

Sprat was not sorry to have a commission in the town. She had been nursing for some days a scheme to go there when she could. She wanted to buy a new nightdress for Ma, who was fretting – in between bouts of fever – over the state of her old one. 'Doctor's coming,' she protested feebly. 'Whatever will he think of me, dressed in this old rag?'

So, just as soon as she had delivered this letter for Miss Raeburn she would put a little more of Gypsy's money to good use. In the meantime, wherever was this house on the address?

She found it – alarmingly – in a little alley, the end of a row with a 'garden' to one side

– a scraggly wilderness of weeds and cats. The woman who opened the door was equally alarming. She was small, but with such a profusion of hair and skirts that she seemed to be twice the ordinary size.

'Come in, come in!' she cried, leading the way into an untidy room where piles of magazines, papers and letters seemed to cover every available surface. Two other women sat at a table: one putting papers into envelopes, the other fitting a new nib to a pen. They nodded and smiled at Sprat as she entered, but did not pause in their work. The new nib was making splatters, Sprat noticed. Pity someone couldn't use a typewriter, like Denzil.

The thought of his name brought crimson to her cheeks and made her sigh faintly.

The woman misinterpreted the sigh. 'You must excuse us, Miss ... Nicholls, did you say it was? Only we are in the act of sending out circulars. You heard what happened in London last Friday?'

Sprat had. It had been the subject of heated argument at Fairviews all weekend. A real premeditated attack on shop windows in the West End. She nodded doubtfully. 'Proper mayhem apparently – stopped the traffic and everything.' Wilful destruction, according to James Raeburn; brave defiance, according to his aunt. 'Made people take notice, I suppose. Though I'm not sure what I make of it, myself.' That was true. She'd always believed in law and order, but she could not help remembering what had happened to Megan.

'Well then,' the woman cried, seizing her by the arm. 'You must have one of our pamphlets, mustn't she, ladies?' She grabbed a copy of the printed circular and thrust it into Sprat's startled hand with her own ink-stained one. There was another smudge, Sprat noticed, on her nose.

The two workers assented enthusiastically. The nib was under control now, and its owner was scribbling away, addressing envelopes.

'You *have* come to join us?' Sprat's usher enquired.

'Not me,' Sprat said hurriedly. 'My employer. And she has sent a donation. It is all in the envelope.'

'Of course,' the woman said. She opened the envelope. 'My word, this is handsome. You would like some tea? No? Then I shall not keep you a moment. I must write a reply at once.' She sat down at a corner of the table in a great flurry of ink and paper, and Sprat found herself obliged to wait.

There was nowhere to sit – all the chairs were covered with piles of paper and *Votes for Women*. That brought back memories. Poor Megan. There seemed to be no relationship between that wretched figure and this odd, enthusiastic group, and she stood there awkwardly until the woman came back and thrust a letter into her hand.

'Here is an acknowledgement for Miss Raeburn. And you must think of joining us yourself. Really you must. Take one of these leaflets, and promise me you'll think about it.'

'I will,' Sprat promised, feeling rather beleaguered. 'Think about, that is.' She took the woman's letter and, laden down with a dozen pamphlets, made her escape.

She was glad to be out of the alley and back in the street. But it was out of the frying pan and into the fire, because, on the corner of Market Jew Street, who should she run into but Norah Roberts.

That was desperately bad luck, since of course Norah couldn't abide to miss anything. But there was no avoiding her.

'Out shopping, m'dear?' Norah said, peering into Sprat's basket and pretending not to.

'Just picking up a few things for Miss Raeburn,' Sprat said quickly. Why hadn't she put those blessed pamphlets out of sight? Well, it was too late now. It was no good trying to disguise anything from Norah.

The woman hitched her cape around her shoulders. 'Much left to get, have you?'

Sprat sighed. She thought of saying something non-committal, but decided against it. You might as well say straight out where you were going or else, wherever you did go, there would be Norah behind you. 'Got to go down to White's Emporium, too, get a new nightdress for Ma.'

At this Norah lost interest in the pamphlets, which she had been trying to study in the basket, upside-down. 'Now isn't that lucky? I've just this minute finished my errands. I'll come in with you, my lover, help you choose. I've known your mother years – I know the sort of thing she likes.'

That was probably true, Sprat thought with a wry grin. If there was a rag duster hanging on the line Norah would know the pattern on it. There was nothing she could say, and Norah *had* been good to Ma lately. 'Dare say you do, at that,' she said, and they went into the Emporium together.

Four

Tom was decidedly unhappy. He had enjoyed his post at Bullivant's, dealing with the front desk and meeting customers – that had been a man's world, and he had been a proper clerk with real expectations. White's Emporium was quite a different matter.

True, he still met the public and he was quite good at that – indeed, that was why Mr White had given him the post. But the clients here were female and they had come, not to dispatch or collect consignments, but to select and purchase clothes and mercery – and that, he found, was something else altogether.

'I'm required,' he complained to his little milliner, the next time they met, 'to stand politely by, doing nothing, for hours, while the ladies fuss about and can't make up their minds.'

'Oh,' she said, dazzled, 'I know. I had a customer...'

He wanted to tell her his woes, not listen to hers. 'Take yesterday for instance. A woman came in for a blouse. First she

138

worried about the buttons. Then it was the hems, and then the finishing. Then she took it to the light to check the colour. She dithered, she dallied, she changed her mind a dozen times and finally took two home "on approval". And what happened? Brought them both back in again today and began all over again.'

'Poor Tom,' the milliner said, stroking his arm, but it didn't make him feel better.

It wasn't just the customers. There was a footling little cash machine on an overhead wire, into which you had to put the docket and the money for purchases. You pulled a cord, and it shuttled off across the shop to the cashier, who would send back the receipt and change. As if, Tom thought, the man at the counter could not be trusted with accounts.

He resented it. He resented having to stand about, looking like a shop-window dummy in his black suit and stiff collar, when there was no one to serve. He resented having to check the stock and wear a flower in his buttonhole. And though White's was an emporium and sold goods 'off the shelf' – with no fitting-room or made-to-measure service – he resented having to carry an inch-tape in his pockets and measure the width of ladies' garments on a counter in full view of the street.

But he could hardly complain. He was

lucky to have a position at all. There had been trouble enough as it was, having to go home and announce that he was 'resigning' from Bullivant's. Fortunately he had been able to blame the strikes – 'Bound to be cutbacks. Better jump before I'm pushed,' he had said – but Father hadn't been pleased.

Mr White wasn't pleased either. There were a lot of angry people who had paid 'premiums' and were demanding their money back. And the carter (who had been given a wigging by Mr Bullivant and lost his contract with the company) had stopped his waggon in the street one night, got out of it, picked Tom up by his lapels and shaken and shouted at him till his teeth rattled.

No, decidedly, Tom Courtney was not a happy man.

His mortification was complete, then, one winter afternoon just before closing, when he turned to greet a pair of customers and found himself face to face with that young lady-friend of Denzil Vargo's. She was in the company of a small stout woman in a preposterous hat, who – though she was not shopping herself – seemed to have appointed herself spokesman for the party.

'Looking for a nightdress, she is,' the woman said with a sniff. 'For her Ma, poor woman, who is in bed with the doctor.'

The girl flashed him an apologetic smile.

'If I could see what you have, please. Do you want to look, Mrs Roberts? I'm not sure what size it would be, exactly...' She broke off. 'Hello! It's Mr Courtney, isn't it? Whatever are you doing here?'

Tom went into his explanation about troubles at Bullivant's. 'Course,' he finished, 'your friend Vargo is all right, with Miss Bullivant to see for him.' He saw the older woman's eyes narrow, and the girl flushed.

'Well, never mind about that,' she said hastily. 'Let's have a look at these nightgowns.'

He summoned one of the shop-girls and had her open the long mahogany drawer marked NIGHTWEAR, LADIES MEDIUM in Indian ink on the label. They were all much of a muchness, white or pink flannelette with acres of flounces and tucks, but this wasn't his department. The female assistants dealt with all ladies' underwear and nightclothes. He might sell an occasional skirt or blouse 'off the peg', but never anything more intimate.

The Nicholls girl went over to examine them while he adopted his mannequin pose near by. The older woman accosted him.

'I hope you're showing her a decent quality. Only the best, she wants. A good girl, she is – not so many young women would inherit a small fortune and lay it out on nightclothes for their Ma. Course, I've known the family for years – good sort of woman, but worried to death, now the doctor's coming, and her without a nightdress fit to be seen.'

Tom was hardly listening, he had his mannequin face on, but something registered in his brain. 'Inherited a fortune, you say?'

The woman looked at him and sucked in her breath. 'Ooh, yes. Got it from her aunt. Rings and jewellery and all sorts. And there's a great house, up here in Penzance, standing empty – it's my belief that'll come to her, by and by. Mind, don't say I said – I aren't supposed to know the half of it, only I went in to give a hand and I happened to see a letter that was behind the clock. Her Ma being so ill and all.'

Tom looked towards Sprat, still assessing the merits of two apparently identical nightgowns. 'Of course.' She was a pretty girl, too.

'Know Sprat well, do you?' the woman said in a voice that suggested that she was well aware that he did.

'I've met her once or twice. When I used to work at Bullivant's.'

'What's this I hear about Vargo, then, getting in with the daughter?'

Tom laughed bitterly. 'You know about that? I'm not surprised; I should think it is all over Penzance. Vargo made a dead set for her – even left home and got himself a room in the house – and she fell for it, like a stone. Of course, Denzil's fallen on his feet. The whole company will come to her one day and he's worked his way in with the father too. Good luck to him, I suppose – but there was no future for the likes of me down there.' Listening to the tale as he told it, he almost believed it himself.

'No,' the woman said, sympathetically. 'They're all the same, these up-overers. Well, it's been nice talking to you. I see Sprat's made her choice over there.' She waddled over. 'Let me have a look, my lover – yes, handsome, that is. But I'd have a bigger size. Good thing you ran into me on the bus. Awful for you, having to do this on your own.'

Tom waited his moment and then carried the parcel, neatly tied with a string handle, and accompanied them to the door. 'Goodnight, ladies. A pleasure to serve you.'

He meant it. He would look out for that Sprat girl. A small fortune, eh?

He was so busy watching her walk up the street that he almost backed into the delivery boy, a grinning lad who had just arrived on his bicycle. Tom scolded him. 'Here, watch where you're going with that machine! Almost knocked me flying.'

The boy's moon-face lit up in a knowing grin. 'Too busy looking at other things, eh,

Mr Courtney? Important customer, is she?'

Tom straightened his tie. 'An heiress,' he said. 'And she thinks a lot of me. So you watch your tongue, young fellow.' He stalked back into the shop with as much dignity as he could muster.

Well, it was true, he thought. And if it wasn't he would make it so. Serve Vargo right for flirting with Olivia so openly that even that woman from the Cove had heard about it from somewhere.

He didn't realise, even then, that she had heard about it from *him*.

'More seed-cake, Denzil?' Mrs Bullivant's hand hovered hospitably over the tea-table. 'Or some buttered loaf, perhaps? We cannot allow our visitors to starve.'

There was little danger of that. These Sunday high teas had become a regular event, and the Bullivants seemed to serve more on each occasion than Denzil could have eaten in a month. Denzil allowed himself to be served with another raisin short-cake and tried to count his blessings.

Olivia was there, dimpled in warm tartan and looking at Denzil with such undisguised approval that, if he had suddenly jumped up and stood on his head in the fireplace, he felt it would scarcely have earned him a frown. His employer, standing before the hearth, was regarding him benevolently too

– though still, Denzil felt, chiefly because he wasn't Tom Courtney.

As for Mrs Bullivant, she was delighted with his company, especially after he expressed an interest in the book she was reading, which he had seen lying open beside her. It was a genuine interest, since the book was the sequel to one that Daisy had brought him from the attic – rather a dull affair, about African missions, but all books were delightful to Denzil.

'Only think of that, Charles,' Mrs Bullivant beamed. 'A young man who is interested in our mission work. You must come with us, one evening, to a meeting. We sometimes have the most fascinating magic-lantern slides.'

Denzil mumbled something courteously non-committal, but Olivia cried, 'Oh, you must. You would enjoy it, I'm sure. There is a mission tea before Christmas, could you not come to that, Denzil – Mr Vargo, that is?' She turned crimson at her own impropriety, and glanced nervously at her papa.

But Bullivant seemed not to have noticed. 'Capital idea,' he said heartily. 'Might not be your sort of affair, Vargo – bread and butter and tea-buns – but if you would care to come with us ..? You could escort Olivia, perhaps.'

Denzil was so surprised that he almost

dropped his shortbread, especially when Daisy – who was presiding with the teapot – caught his eye behind the others' backs and gave him an enormous wink. (What had Sprat once said to him? 'You're in with a chance there. Court her and be happy.') He managed to murmur, 'I should be honoured, sir,' and the matter was settled.

Olivia turned more scarlet than ever and looked delighted; Mrs Bullivant nodded and smiled; and her husband hmmphed, clearly pleased.

Denzil found the courage to say, 'I wonder, under the circumstances, whether I might be permitted to go to St Evan next Sunday, sir, to visit my mother? I have not seen her for some time, and I should like to see her before Christmas.'

Bullivant looked at him. 'St Evan? Is that where your mother lives? I thought I had heard another name.'

Denzil smiled. 'Penvarris. Yes indeed, sir. But I thought to see her at the church. My father has returned home from abroad, and we do not...' he hesitated, '... see eye to eye.' He remembered that the Bullivants were chapelgoers, and he added with a flash of inspiration, 'On the subject of alcohol, for instance. He is, I fear, a little too fond of it.'

Mrs Bullivant regarded him warmly. 'Your father is prey to the demon drink? You poor young man. I had wondered why you never sought to visit your family, but now I understand, of course. How dreadful for you.' She brightened. 'You could not, I suppose, be persuaded to take him a pamphlet from the Band of Hope?'

Denzil could imagine only too clearly what Father would do with a temperance tract, let alone the person who tried to give him one, but he managed to keep a straight face and evade the offer without offending.

'But of course you must visit your mother,' Mrs Bullivant continued. 'It is so long since you have seen her – not since that fearful accident. And you were so brave, too. Tell us again, how did it happen, that dreadful business with the horse?'

'Nothing to tell,' Denzil said hastily, and was obliged to turn the conversation to converting the Zulus.

But the die was cast. He was to go to St Evan next Sunday to see Mother (he would drop a note to the vicar when he forwarded the rent) and a fortnight later he was to escort Miss Bullivant to the Christmas Mission Tea.

Ma was dimly pleased to have the nightdress, though by the time it arrived she was almost too weak and feverish to know much about it. She seemed to have got worse over the last few weeks.

Mrs Polmean's diagnosis had been right,

to Pa's astonishment and grief, and the doctor had given Ma some kind of medicine, 'to get rid of things', as he said. But though the mixture had crucified her with pain and cramps, it hadn't had the desired effect, and the doctor had to be called a second time. He had come out looking graver than ever.

'Says there's nothing for it, my handsome, he'll 'ave to operate, or we'll lose her,' Pa said when Sprat went down next evening to see how she was (the ladies at Fairviews had been wonderful, giving her time off every afternoon). It would mean less pay, of course (and her bit of money was needed, with Ma so ill), but lots of employers wouldn't be half so good. She might have had to leave work and come home altogether, and things would have been awfully tight then.

So here she was in the kitchen, making tea and listening to Pa. He was looking stricken, as if he could do with a drop of something stronger. There was some brandy open on the dresser: Ma, who was terrified at her unexpected condition and even more terrified of the operation, had been given some to help her sleep. But when Sprat suggested it to Pa he shook his head.

'I'll do, my handsome. It's your ma you want to be worried for. No cutting involved, the doctor 'splained to me, but she'll have to have chloroform. Coming tomorrow, he is, and bringing a nurse with him. Wants the kitchen table scrubbed down with disinfectant and carbolic, clean sheets for her to go to and a pile of hot water for his hands.' Pa looked woeful and helpless. 'Don't know who I can ask. Mrs Polmean, d'you think?'

So Sprat spent the evening scrubbing the table till her hands were raw, and finding the best sheets from the chest. Only used for Mrs Mason, generally, but this was different, and even Ma's feeble protests were overruled. Sprat was glad she had bought the nightgown, finest quality, with little ribbon bows. 'Good enough to be buried in,' Norah had said, rather tactlessly. By now it would be the gossip of the Cove.

'Now then,' Sprat said, pouring another good strong cup of tea for Pa, 'want me down here, do you, while the doctor's here?'

Pa shook his head. 'There'll be a nurse here, and Mrs Polmean – good as gold, she's been, offering to come in. I think your Ma will be relieved to have her. Nothing much that you and I can do, my lover. I'm thinking to be off down the yard for a bit, keep out the way. Best if you do the same. Your ma'd be mortified if she thought we'd seen her in that state.'

That was true, Sprat thought. Ma was fiercely private – the thought of this operation must make her squirm. It showed how ill she was, or she wouldn't have stood for it. So Sprat stayed away, and the next afternoon when she arrived it was all over. The kitchen smelled horribly of chloroform, Mrs Polmean had scrubbed the tabletop again, and Ma was tucked up in the best sheets, wearing her new nightdress and being pathetically sick into the washbowl.

Sprat had expected somehow that the operation would have immediate results; but Ma looked iller than ever and the terrible fever was raging on. Pa was beside her bed, wringing out cold cloths for her forehead, but Ma seemed scarcely conscious of their presence. She dozed, retched, moaned faintly and dozed again. Sprat was conscious of a kind of panic.

'How is she?'

Pa looked up piteously. 'Doctor's pleased, Sprat. Went as well as can be expected, he says, but it's touch and go even now. Ice, we need, to bring the fever down. But where do you find ice round here, that's the thing?'

Sprat put on her bonnet again. 'I dunno,' she said. 'But I'll find out. I believe they have some down Newlyn, don't they, for the fish?'

'Here,' Pa said. 'It's pouring with rain. And it'll be dark in an hour. You can't go out Newlyn looking for ice this time of day.'

But she did.

Five

They did indeed have ice at Newlyn, and were willing to sell her some, a cut lump of it, which was not altogether what Sprat had expected. Neither had she stopped to consider how she might get it home.

The fellow at the iceworks was very good when he heard her story, wrapping her ice-block in layers and layers of newspapers and even lending her a bucket to carry it, but Sprat could see that privately he was half laughing at her plight. No insulated box, no cork or kapok wrappings, and no chance of a bus ride home – how could she be such a chump? It was a long way to Penvarris, especially in the rain, and if she didn't hurry up with it she stood a good chance of arriving home soaked to the skin with only a bucket of cold water to show for her efforts.

It would be getting dark soon, too, and she set off back along the road as fast as she could manage, even breaking at times into an unladylike gallop. But that didn't help, she was getting breathless, and the parcel in the bucket was already melting. She slowed to a walk again, feeling cross and ridiculous, when a voice from behind her called, 'Miss Nicholls?'

She turned, expecting a familiar face. Crowdie perhaps, on his way home from the town with the cart – that would have been a blessing indeed.

But it was not Crowdie, it was a young man on a delivery bicycle, which he was piloting, Sprat thought, with no particular skill. He drew up beside her and doffed his cap, and she saw to her surprise that it was the young man from the Emporium – the one who had been at Bullivant's and bought her an ice-cream once.

'Hello,' she said. 'Whatever are you doing on that bicycle? Pop up everywhere, you do, like a jack-in-a-box.'

He grinned triumphantly, 'Borrowed it off the delivery boy – I wasn't going to walk home this weather, if I could help it. Early closing today. We've finished at the shop.' He was about to dismount, she saw with alarm. 'Saw you from the corner – I thought it was you.'

She smiled hesitantly. 'Well, nice of you, but I can't stop. I got to get this here ice home to my mother before it melts. Missed the early bus, too, and if I wait for the next one the dratted stuff will melt. Melt in any case, most likely, before I get it home.'

Tom looked at her, laughing. 'What are

you doing with ice, anyway?'

She told him, and his smile died. 'Oh yes, of course, your mother. I remember. You bought a nightdress for her from the shop.' He looked up suddenly, grinning. 'Wait! I've got an idea. What about this machine?'

Sprat stared. 'What am I supposed to do with it? I can't ride a bicycle.'

'I can,' he said. 'You sit on the bar, I'll pedal. It'll be miles quicker than walking.'

'You're mad,' she said with conviction. It was a solution of a kind, but it was out of the question. Nice girls didn't ride about on crossbars, not even with young men they had known all their lives. As for doing it with a near-stranger! You might as well write 'Fallen Woman' on a label and pin it to your forehead.

Tom looked crestfallen. 'This is an emergency,' he said. 'Your ice'll melt. I mean it. I'm only trying to help.'

'Ride out there and back?' she said. 'At this hour? In the rain?'

'Pleased to do it,' he said. 'For you. With your mother ill and all.'

'If you really want to help,' she said slowly, 'you could take it for me. I'll tell you where to go, and I can take the horse-bus.' She saw the look on his face and added, 'I'll pay you for going, of course, don't worry. I got a bit of money coming to me.'

He seemed to be debating with himself.

'All right,' he said at last. 'Give that bucket here.' He put it on the handlebars. He hesitated again and then said, 'And forget about the money. If you want to pay me, you can do it by going for a walk with me. Down the Promenade, perhaps, one of these Sunday afternoons. What do you say?'

She found herself smiling. 'You *are* mad!'

'Mad for you,' he said. 'Ever since I saw you first. Now, tell me where to take this ice, before it's too late.'

She told him, and he set off, wobbling. She half believed he wouldn't get there, but when she arrived herself, a good ninety minutes later, she found him in the kitchen at the Row, drinking tea. He'd managed to deliver the ice, and Pa had broken it up and applied it to Ma's brow. It seemed to have done the trick, too, Pa said. Ma was sleeping quietly, and Mrs Polmean was upstairs sitting with her.

'That young man's drying off before he sets off back,' Pa explained to Sprat in a penetrating whisper as she took off her wet things in the hall. 'Poor lad, he came off his bike on the hill, and now he'll have to walk all the way home because he's got no lights. Good of him to come all this way, for us.' He smiled meaningfully at her – the first time she had seen him smile in weeks. 'Asked if he could take you walking one Sunday, and I've said yes, if you can get

154

away. Interesting fellow.'

Sprat hadn't thought of him as 'interesting', but she soon saw what Pa meant. When she came downstairs from seeing Ma, Tom was talking to Pa with great animation about pilot-gigs. Apparently he was very keen on boats.

The meeting with Mother was not what Denzil had expected. He had sent her word through the vicar that he was coming, and he had expected a joyful reunion. He was disappointed.

Mother was waiting for him in the church porch. There was a little carved bench-seat there, and she had perched herself on it, awkward in her Sunday best. She looked up when she saw him.

'You've come then?' Straight-faced.

He sat down beside her. 'I said I would.'

'Yes.'

He tried to take her hand but she pulled it away. He realised that she was trembling. He said, 'Your rent going through all right?'

'Yes.' Pause. 'You're some good, Denzil. And looking well. The Bullivants are good to you?'

'Very good.' Why was she so distant? 'And I'm doing well in the office. A fellow left, and I got a bit of a promotion.' She would be pleased with that, she was always so proud of his office work.

'Glad of that, then.'

He tried for the hand again, and she snatched it away urgently. 'Don't do that. Folks might be watching. I'll be in trouble enough as it is if your father finds out.'

So that was it! He said, tenderly, 'How are you, Mother?'

She looked at him helplessly. 'In purgatory, that's what. He's a monster, that man. What possessed me to marry him I don't know. Bad enough then, but now he's ten times worse. No work, that's the half of it. He's up St Just most days, just carrying parcels or holding horses for a few pence. Only of course I never see it. Minute he's got money, he's down the public house spending it – or looking for an argument, more like. Wonder he hasn't been had up. Then coming in all hours, roaring and bellowing at me for not having his meal waiting. And when it *is* ready he doesn't like it. But I can't give him what I haven't got, Denzil, and that's a fact. Wish there were a few more like Crowdie, who had the sense to pay him with a bit of something to eat. All right, we were, when he was working there.'

'But that's over?'

She sighed. 'Seasonal, it was. Crowdie's good but he can't invent work, and there's nothing down the mines and factories – they're laying people off with these strikes, not taking them on, even if they don't smell

156

of drink.'

'Perhaps he can go back to Crowdie in the spring,' Denzil said.

'It's to be hoped so. Crowdie's the only person your father seems to take any notice of. But I don't know. They fell out over something – your father won't tell me what – months ago, and he's avoided Crowdie ever since. Whatever it is, it's got your father worried. Won't say a word about it, even when he's drunker 'n a bull.'

Denzil nodded. 'Might be that Sprat Nicholls business. You heard about that? Father grabbed hold of her in the lane, apparently, shook her about and threatened her. Terrified her. Poor girl screamed her head off, till Crowdie and that Mr Raeburn came and rescued her.'

Mother was shaking her head in horror. 'Your father attacked her? The man wants locking up. I've got no time for that Nicholls family myself, but there's no excuse for that!' She examined her hands in their home-made gloves. 'Perhaps that was it. Your father never said. Maybe he was too ashamed of hisself, for once.'

Denzil frowned. Mother wasn't one for talking, as a rule, but she was talking now, and he dared a question he had been wanting to ask for a long time. 'What is it you've got against Sprat's family exactly? Mrs Nicholls is a bit of a battleaxe, I know, but

157

there's plenty worse, and Pincher seems nice enough.'

Mother sat up straight and pursed her lips. 'Things!' she said primly.

'Well,' Denzil said, 'if you won't tell me you won't, but I don't know how I'm supposed to conduct myself when I'm only told half a tale. My father lays violent hands on a girl, and hollers like a bull when he hears her name, but I'm not allowed to know why. I'd have married her, given half a chance, Father or not – but she won't have me now and who's to blame her?' His voice shook as he spoke.

His mother looked at him. 'It's the fault of those Jenkins girls, if you must know. Myrtle Nicholls and her sister. Split up the Vargo family – or rather Gypsy did. She was a friend of mine, you remember, and that was bad enough – her being a Cover and me being from the village – but after I married Stan ... well.'

She paused, and Denzil had to prompt her. 'Go on.'

'She got to meet his brother Billy, that's what. Well, that was it. Like iron filings to a magnet. Nothing would do but they should walk out together. Nice-looking boy Billy was, too, and that smitten! And Gypsy Nicholls was as smart as paint. Working down Major Selwood's big house in Penzance, she was, and turned herself out something lovely. But the village didn't like it, with her being from the Cove. Course things were different then – people took their differences serious.'

It hadn't changed much, Denzil thought, but he said nothing.

Ma sighed. 'There was no end of trouble. He and Stan came to blows over it. Billy got spat on down the mine. Men from the Cove came up here threatening him. But Billy wouldn't heed. Gone mad for her, he was – and she was worse. Left home and went into service in town, just so she could meet him – or so she said.'

Like himself and Sprat.

'Then one evening Billy came home, white as chalk, and said it was all over. Called Stan every name under the sun, packed up his things and walked out. We never saw him again. Then, years later, we had a letter from Canada saying Stan was right and he'd been wrong, and Gypsy was a pile of trouble. He'd made a new life and married a woman he met out there. Doing handsome, he said, and plenty of work for all.'

Denzil nodded.

'Course, Stan couldn't keep his mouth shut. Always wants to be proved right. He went down the mine telling everybody, until one of the captains said something he didn't like – accused Billy of leaving Gypsy in the lurch, instead of vice versa – and your father

159

laid him out with a pick-handle. Start of all our troubles, that was, and of course your father blamed me because Gypsy was my friend to start with.' She looked at Denzil bleakly. 'And you know, she never spoke to me again. So you see, Denzil, it's like I say – any trouble for a Vargo, and there's a Jenkins at the back of it.'

Denzil winced. It was worse than he'd thought. This was not just the village's usual mistrust of anyone from the Cove; Sprat's family had been directly responsible for Father losing his job all that time ago and for all those years of struggle. Not to mention the bitter family quarrels, the betrayals, and generally making the Vargos the talk of the district. No wonder Father was furious when he heard about Sprat. He said glumly, 'But that was then...'

'And this is now,' his mother said. 'And you are the image of Billy and she's the spit of her aunt. It's like seeing the two of them together again.' She sighed. 'There! Now I've told you. Just don't tell your father, that's all. He won't have her name mentioned in the house – or yours either.' She stood up heavily. 'Good to see you, son. I'm glad you're well. Have a nice Christmas, you hear? Only we better not meet any more. More than my life's worth, if your father knew I was here.'

He hesitated. 'Mother...'

She shook her head. 'Time I went home, see if he's chopped up any more of the furniture for firewood. Don't come home, Denzil, it'd break your heart to see what we've come to.'

Denzil felt in his pocket. He had brought a half-crown to give her, but her last words wrung his heart. He had a sovereign in his pocket, destined for the tallyman – with his new position he could afford to pay off a bit for his clothes. He took out both coins and dropped them in her palm.

'Happy Christmas, Mother,' and he left quickly, so as not to see her tears.

Tom got his Sunday walk with Sprat in the end, but he had to work hard for it. You would almost think the girl was unwilling to come, though her father had seemed pleased as Punch at the suggestion.

Granted, there were difficulties. It had to be a Sunday, for a start, because White's opened late most nights and didn't finish early on a Saturday. But of course there was no bus on a Sunday – and Wilhemina (he couldn't call her by that ridiculous nickname!) protested that it was much too far to walk. It *was* a long way too, much further than he had expected when he'd volunteered to ride out there in the rain on that confounded bicycle.

Of course he had never told her the truth

of that – just let her suppose it was chance that he had 'happened' to be passing. In fact it was nothing of the sort. Tom had been closing up that day when the delivery boy sauntered up, smiling all over his suet-pudding face.

'What are you smirking at?'

'Seen your heiress, haven't I? Drenched half to death. Down to Newlyn outside the iceworks. That where she works, is it? Or what's she heiress to?' He grinned at his own impudence, keeping out of range.

Tom ignored this. He put up the last of the shutters and pulled the bolts. 'When was this?' He was calculating fast.

'Five minutes ago; I've just come from there.'

Tom turned towards him, and the boy ducked, but instead of giving him a clout round the ear Tom seized the bicycle from under his astonished nose and pedalled off as fast he could. On purpose to catch her, naturally, and find some excuse to engage her in conversation.

Which he had done, very successfully. Got himself soaking wet in the process, but put her under an obligation and made a good impression on the father.

According to Tom's ideas of natural justice, it should have been easy after that, but in fact it wasn't. The walk was arranged only after a long negotiation. The father remembered that there was a carol concert at the bandstand one Sunday, where the local male-voice choir were singing, so Wilhemina could get a lift in and out again on the cart. Tom's ideas about walking her part-way home and stealing a sly kiss were drearily dispelled.

The weather was dreary too, when the day came. A grey, damp, cheerless day with never a chink in the clouds, although at least it didn't actually rain. Sprat arrived muffled to the eyebrows in a great thick scarf and coat and a black bonnet – her mother's, she said – and looked like someone brought in from the Salvation Army. Still, she had a pretty face – and a pretty figure under all those wrappings. He reminded himself of the small fortune and the big house in Penzance, and set out to charm her as much as possible.

She wasn't hard to entertain. Afternoon walks on the Promenade were new to her, and she obviously enjoyed the experience, even if it was mid-winter. He pointed out the rocks and landmarks, with more confidence than accuracy, and she was impressed by that. She wanted to stop and hear the carols, too, to Tom's secret irritation, and he was obliged to stand miserably in the damp and cold, shifting from one foot to the other and smiling encouragingly every time she looked in his direction.

However, it had the desired effect. Little by little she returned his smiles, and by the end of the afternoon, when he had to deliver her back to the cart, she allowed him to take her by the elbows and swing her up, laughing, on to the step. For a dizzying moment she leaned against him, and he was aware of her body, even under the folds of coat.

He stood there holding her hand. She didn't pull it away. 'We must do this again,' he said.

'Next time there's a carol concert.' She was teasing him.

'When the weather's better. In the spring.'

She laughed, disengaging her fingers. 'Maybe.'

'In the meanwhile, any time you come into town, you come into White's, you hear? You want anything in the store, I'll look out for you.' The driver had folded up the step and she was sitting down in the back of the cart, muffled under a rug with the male-voice singers. Tom added urgently, 'All right?'

'All right.' She waved a gloved hand at him, and called, as the cart set off, 'Thank you for a nice afternoon.'

And with that he had to be content.

Six

Denzil had never been to a chapel tea before – let alone a 'Special Sunday Afternoon Christmas Tea in Aid of Missions' – and he was not at all sure what he should expect. In fact it was a simple, staid affair, held not in the chapel at all, but in the Sunday-school hall, where rows of long trestle tables had been piled with iced buns, saffron cake and mincemeat pies, and piles of buttered splits spread with egg and cress or (because it was a special occasion) salmon paste. Nothing hot, Mrs Bullivant explained, because it was Sunday, although the ladies had provided a cup of tea and there was lemonade for the children.

Denzil 'escorted' Olivia, meaning that he showed her to a chair, fetched her tea and then sat beside her as they listened to a visiting missionary who talked, with passion and illustrated slides, about the mission to the Zulus and how it had been affected by the South African War. It was interesting stuff, but some of the stories – the customs of the natives, and the privations of our own internment camps – were enough to put a man completely off his iced buns.

Olivia, though, was radiant – 'Isn't that wonderful?' – and people were very kind, wishing to be introduced to Denzil and urging him with the greatest friendliness to attend again. 'We always have special services at Christmas,' said a man who seemed to be a sort of preacher, though he was not a clergyman.

And Denzil – thinking of his mother shivering in a pew at St Evan while Father roistered somewhere in a fury – was glad to thank these simple, good-natured, abstemious folk and promise to come back.

Then there were hymns and prayers, and the children sang carols. Some of the women took away the dishes (to the disapproval of some of the older folk, who 'didn't hold with washing up on the Sabbath'), and the Sunday school performed a nativity, with the help of a good many striped towels and a china-doll Jesus. This caused a tiny stir when Mary accidentally dropped it off the stage, but it was promptly rescued ('Ooops!') and wiped on the sleeve of one of the wise men, who must have been at least four years old. It was enchanting. Denzil was quite sorry when it was over.

There was a collection in aid of the mission, and there were more hymns and more prayers – people seemed to make them up where they stood – and then it was time to drive home in a cab through the darkening streets. The Bullivants were in a hurry because they had to go home and get ready for evening chapel, where the earnest missionary was speaking again. Olivia was pressing in her invitations for Denzil to accompany them.

Denzil shook his head, laughing – privately feeling that one afternoon of Zulus was quite enough for the average man – but when the hansom turned the corner on to the Promenade something happened which made the smile die on his lips.

There was a cart, parked beside the pavement, and a group of people were climbing into it. Carol singers by the look of it – several of them had instrument cases and sheet-music – and Denzil might not have spared them a second glance.

It was Olivia who spoke. 'Only look, Papa. Isn't that Tom Courtney over there?'

Denzil saw him then, talking to a girl in a big bonnet and a scarf. They walked to the cart and Tom seized the girl and lifted her like a feather on to the step, and she stood there laughing down at him.

'Somebody likes him, at any rate,' Denzil said, and then, as the girl stood there, leaning down from the step with her hand in Tom's, Denzil saw who it was. It was Sprat. Sprat! He had not even known that she was back from London.

He swallowed. 'Yes,' he said suddenly to Olivia. 'Yes, I'd love to come to the service with you. If you will make allowances for my churchy ways.'

'Of course,' she said, glowing. 'And don't worry. I'll be there to hold your hand.' She flushed. 'Metaphorically, of course.'

But adoration is appealing, and before the new year was very old he was holding her hand in fact.

Mr Raeburn's modest evening party was quite a success.

A man called Major Selwood and his wife had come up for the evening – more to see the inside of Fairviews than anything, Sprat guessed – and the whole place had seemed to come alive. There had been an 'atmosphere' in the house lately, between Mr Raeburn and his aunt, and Sprat was secretly relieved that arrangements for the occasion seemed to have thawed their conversations a little.

Of course, the evening 'wasn't anything special', at least according to Fitch and Florrie, who took turns at boasting of the wonderful parties and entertainments their various employers had held in London at one time and another. Cook glanced at Sprat, raised her eyebrows and went on preparing a salmon galantine. It all seemed special enough to Sprat.

Mr Raeburn had sent away for a wonderful machine, a 'gramophone', which had a little cylinder and played a tune when you wound it up. Miss Raeburn had been severe with him over it – it cost no end, and then it had to be sent – but it proved to be the success of the evening. Mrs Selwood was enchanted with it, and – since you could change the tune by changing the cylinder – there was music all the evening even without a piano.

Sprat had found herself unexpectedly the focus of another kind of attention. She had been required to help serve at supper, although most of the duties had fallen to Fitch, who had positively revelled in the opportunity, swooping around effortlessly in a neat black uniform jacket and trousers with a stripe at the seam, which made him look as dashing as an etching. It was Sprat, though, who captured the attention of the Selwoods – or in any case of Major Selwood – though she rather wished that she hadn't. He was a big, bluff, hearty man, who eyed her most intently when he first arrived and drew her over at the first opportunity, to ask her all about herself. Sprat didn't know how to answer. She told him as little as she could and escaped downstairs in embarrassment as soon as she was able.

The evening did not go on very late, on

the instructions of Nurse Bloom, and by half past ten the Selwoods had gone home. Mr Raeburn, flushed with the success of his gramophone, had – as a special treat – allowed Fitch to bring it downstairs for the servants. They wound it up. Fitch seized Florrie by the waist and danced around the kitchen with her, to the huge delight of Sprat and Cook, until Nurse Bloom came down and spoke to them severely for making too much noise.

'Mr Raeburn and Mrs Meacham have had a busy day. They need their rest – without the interruption of galumphing from the kitchen.' And they had sheepishly turned it off and gone about finishing their chores.

In fact, that party was the better part of Christmas. Ma was a little better: the fever had eased and she was no longer in pain, but she had no more strength than a spider. Sometimes when you spoke to her she was Ma, and sometimes she wasn't. The doctor – called in again at a guinea a visit – said that she was 'progressing, although there are still poisons in her blood', but there was nothing he could give her except soothing drinks and something to make her sleep, and Sprat could see that it was going to be a long, long time before Ma was properly herself again.

Pa looked red-eyed and worn, and though he was starting to go down the yard or out with the pots again – while Mrs Polmean watched Ma – his heart wasn't in it. 'Anyway,' he grumbled, 'it's a poor time of year for fishing, and you can't build boats in this weather.' Sprat's heart ached for him.

Mrs Meacham was very good to Sprat, and let her go down with her presents the minute they got back from church. A new woollen vest for Pa (lovingly knitted by candlelight over many evenings), and for Ma a pair of hand-made fleecy drawers, of a design that Mrs Pritchard insisted was called 'nickybuggers' until Florrie had shrieked, 'It's knickerbockers!' and laughed till she cried.

Miss Raeburn had even looked out an old nightdress 'for your mother', a beautiful thing in softest pink Vyella with embroidered roses at the yoke. Ma's pale eyes lit up at the sight of it, and even Pa joked that they would have to wash it straight off, and get it on the line so Norah could admire it.

There were presents waiting at the Cove too. A hanky for Sprat ('It isn't much, my lover, but you know how things are') and, to her surprise, a small oblong box wrapped up in brown paper – 'To the Nicholls family, with hopes for a speedy recovery and best wishes for Christmas'.

Sprat looked at Pa.

'From that young man of yours.' For a moment Sprat's heart leapt, thinking of

Denzil, but Pa's next words put paid to that idea. 'Came down here again on his bicycle with it.' He smiled. 'Aren't you going to open it?'

Sprat tore off the wrapping almost crossly. The cheek of that Tom Courtney, sending down presents to people he hardly knew!

'My heaven!' Pa said. 'Whatever's that? Chocolates?'

It was. A whole little box of them. No wonder Pa was surprised. People in the Row didn't have boxes of chocolates – they cost at least sixpence, and you could feed a man for a week on less than that.

Sprat sat there foolishly, holding the box. 'Don't know how he thought this would help Ma,' she said, knowing that she sounded ungracious.

Pa looked at her sharply. 'Thought it would cheer us up, more than like.'

Sprat put the box on the table, unopened. 'Well, it's a kind thought, I suppose, but if he thought that, he's mistaken. Take more than a few sweets to cheer me up this Christmas. You have one if you want – they're addressed to us all. Don't feel like it myself, and I'll have to be getting back.' She sounded sour and she knew it, so she bent over and kissed his head. 'Thank you for the handkerchief.'

'Don't know why you're so down on that young man of yours,' he said. 'Seemed a nice gesture to me.'

'Seems a bit untoward to me,' Sprat retorted. 'He isn't really my young man, either. More your friend than mine, if anything, with all your chatting about boats. And I aren't down on him, exactly. It's just … he isn't my young man, that's all.'

And she left. She could have kicked herself afterwards – things were bad enough at the Row without her making them worse – but somehow at the time she couldn't help it. Proper pest, that Tom Courtney. It wasn't that she was 'down on him', exactly – he was quite nice when he tried. But he wasn't Denzil, perhaps that was it – and the poor fellow could hardly help that.

She felt so guilty that the following week she wrote him a letter thanking him for his gift – merely a polite acknowledgement, just as she had always been brought up to write thank-you notes to Gypsy. She wasn't to know that Tom Courtney would take it as encouragement, and start to borrow that bicycle again.

PART THREE

March 1912 – June 1913

One

Tom was delighted when Sprat walked into the Emporium one afternoon. She hadn't been back into the shop since the day of the nightdress, though he had been urging her ever since to come again. Partly he wanted her to see him like this – in his buttonhole and suit, looking a little important – but mostly it saved him having to go trailing out to the Cove.

He had done it once or twice, on the borrowed bicycle, but he hated the place: the cramped, mean little house, and Pincher Nicholls boring him for hours with his dreary talk of boat-building. And even then it was all Sprat would do to walk up to the top road with him and let him slip a sly hand around her waist.

What would his family say if they knew? He had told them that he was trying to court a girl with expectations, but he hadn't told them the rest of it: illiterate parents, dreadful little dwellings, horrible prying neighbours and the smell of fish.

So it was a stroke of luck, her being here

today. He came forward with his best professional smile. 'Can I be of service, miss?'

She gave him a withering smile. 'Don't be so daft, Tom. Though as a matter of fact you *can* help me. Mrs Meacham wants some more of those white towels – same as she had last time. Nurse Bloom *will* have them boiled every week and they don't last.'

Tom led the way importantly to the 'household mercery' and spread out one of the towels on the counter. 'Is this what you require?' She put her hand out to feel it and he covered it with his own, out of sight of the other assistants. 'Beautiful and soft,' he said, stroking her fingers, 'just what you want against your skin.'

It was daring, pretending to talk about the towels like that, and her face softened into a grin. 'I'll have two of those, please, Mr Courtney,' she said, and he heard her suppress a giggle as he put his other hand on hers. She moved it swiftly. 'And you can wrap them up. I'm to take them with me.'

She was quick-witted, for a girl. He took the towels and made a neat package of them. 'To be charged to Mrs Meacham's account? Certainly. And now I'll carry this for you and escort you to the door.'

When they reached the street she said, mock-severely, 'You're a caution, you are, Tom Courtney. How am I supposed to shop with you carrying on like that?'

He countered with a compliment. Girls liked that, he'd learned – or at least the little milliner did. 'How am I supposed to concentrate on working with you looking like that?'

It worked. She blushed and smiled. 'Get away with you. Here, give me that parcel, it'll go in here if I move these papers.' She scuffled around in the bottom of her basket and made room for the towels.

'What are those? Pamphlets from the Women's Movement! Mind you don't get arrested.'

'They are for Miss Raeburn.' She shrugged. 'Can't be arrested for reading pamphlets.'

'I don't know so much. Mr White was speaking to a policeman; they've got nine thousand officers on the street of London today. There have been threats of more outbreaks of window-smashing. Hundreds of arrests, they're expecting. Anyone who looks like a sympathiser. So you be careful. Where would your mother be without you? Or me, for that matter. How is your family, by the way? The boat coming on?'

'Almost finished,' Sprat said. 'Better be, too. Pa's hoping to launch it next week. Highest tide of the year, with it being the equinox.'

Tom tried to look as if he knew what that

meant. 'Might come down and see it,' he said. 'Your father asked me.'

'Well, wear old clothes and stout boots if you do,' Sprat said. 'All hands to the ropes, it'll be. But Pa'd be pleased. Just hope it's all ready in time. There's some rigging rope hasn't arrived yet. I would pop into Bullivant's and ask, but...' She stopped.

'You don't want to run into Vargo?'

She nodded. 'I've hardly spoken to him since he moved into town – and that was before I went to London. When I did...'

Tom watched her closely. 'It's that Olivia Bullivant,' he said carefully. 'He's made a dead set at her, you know. And of course, she thinks he's a hero. Ever since he stopped that runaway horse, or whatever he did.'

She was staring at him. 'What runaway horse?'

She didn't know! That was interesting. Surely news like that would have been the talk of Penvarris when it happened? He said, 'When he had his face knocked in – you must have heard? He was a terrible mess.'

Sprat was looking aghast. 'A runaway horse! Poor Denzil. I'd no idea. Is he all right now?

Tom shrugged. 'I should think so. I haven't seen him for ages.' He couldn't resist turning the screw. 'Too busy with his new friends.'

Suppose, he thought to himself, there never was a runaway horse? What then? And if not, what had caused those injuries? A brawl? Wouldn't Bullivant love that! He smiled. It shouldn't be too difficult to find out.

Sprat walked sharply up the street. Denzil, kicked by a runaway horse! Why, people had been killed with less than that. When had that happened? she wondered. While she was in London, no doubt. Poor Denzil; she hoped he was all right.

Well, she did have business in Bullivant's – or at the very least an excuse to call. She marched up and through the door before she had time to change her mind.

She saw him as soon as she went in, at the front counter, where Tom Courtney used to be. He wasn't a mess at all, in fact he was looking better than last time she saw him. His face was blotchy *then*, she remembered. Perhaps that was the horse? But he would have said, surely? Or Norah would have, if he didn't.

He looked up and saw her. 'Good-morning.' If icicles could talk, Sprat thought, they would sound just like that. 'If you have come in about that consignment, Miss Nicholls, I'm afraid it has not yet arrived.'

She glared at him. 'Well, I did and I didn't.' How could he be so perverse? 'I came in to see how you were. Heard you had an argument with a horse – but it's all nonsense, I can see.'

He looked around nervously. 'Look,' he said, 'keep your voice down.'

She did so, astonished. 'What's the matter?'

He leaned towards her. 'You know what's the matter. I'm sorry about what happened, but I don't know why you have to come in here, making trouble.'

'Making trouble!' She forgot to whisper for a moment. 'Tom Courtney told me you been kicked by a horse, so I came to ask after you. How's that causing trouble?'

He looked exasperated. 'Because there never was a horse,' he said in a low voice. 'I got that black eye from fighting Father, as you very well know.'

'Fighting him? Denzil, you didn't? Not over what he said to me? Calling me a...' she couldn't bring herself to say 'bastard'; '... a relation?' she finished lamely.

Denzil was looking at her as if she was mad. 'A relation? Who to?'

She found herself looking at him in the same way. 'To you, of course. Denzil, what is this about?'

He came around the counter and seized her by the arm. 'Say that again! My father said you were related to me?'

It was her turn to say, 'Sssh!' and glance

182

around. 'People'll hear.'

'Bullivant's out,' Denzil said. 'Here, come in the inner office.' He opened the door. 'Claude – I need to talk to this customer, urgent. You come out and keep an eye on the desk, and if anyone comes, call me. All right?'

'Yes, Mr Vargo,' and Claude went out, shining with responsibility.

Denzil shut the door again. 'Now then, sit on that stool and tell me from the beginning.'

Sprat looked at him helplessly. 'But Denzil, you already know! Isn't that why you left Penvarris?'

'I left because I came to blows with my father. He came in drunk, threatening me and Mother, and I ... well, I'm not proud of it but I knocked him out with a skillet. I couldn't go home after that, he'd have half killed me. I wrote to you about it.'

'I never got it. There was fever in the house.'

'But ... when he threatened you ... you told me you knew!'

'No,' she said simply. 'I didn't know *that*. All I knew was, he stopped me in the lane, and called me a...' She couldn't say it.

'A what?'

She took the plunge. 'A bastard.' She saw the shock register on Denzil's face. 'Worst of it is, Denzil, it's true. I aren't Ma's daughter at all, it turns out – I'm Gypsy's.' Tears were running down her face again, and she couldn't stop them. 'Your Uncle Billy, it seems – only, when he heard he pushed off to Canada and wouldn't marry her.'

He looked astonished. 'That's not what Mother says. She says Billy was torn to pieces because Gypsy wouldn't have *him*. Never said a word about you.'

Sprat shook her head. 'She didn't know, perhaps. Isn't a thing to shout from the housetops. But Billy knew. Offered money to marry her, he was, and still wouldn't do it.' She sighed. 'So now you know, Denzil. We're cousins, at best – and if it wasn't Billy it must have been your Pa, and that's even worse. Either way your family was the ruin of mine, and they'd never forgive either of us – my Ma had to be nearly dying before she'd forgive her closest friend for an argument! So where does that leave us?'

But Denzil wasn't listening. 'Offered him money? Who did?'

'I dunno.' Sprat was startled. 'Gypsy, I suppose. Someone did. And it's not imagination. Your father knew about it. It was one of the things he was calling after me, in the lane. Still...' But she never finished. There was a rap on the door. Claude stuck his head around.

'Mr Bullivant,' he said, urgently, 'coming in, this minute.'

They hardly had time to get into the outer office before Mr Bullivant entered, with Olivia on his arm. Denzil said breathlessly, 'Should be here by next week at the latest, Miss Nicholls.'

Sprat knew she was flushed, but had the presence of mind to reply, 'Well, I do hope so, Mr Vargo. My father is hoping to launch the boat by then. I'll look in again. Good-day.'

She was almost glad when she met Norah on the bus, and had to hear about what Mrs Polmean had said to the butcher. It prevented her from having to think about other things too much.

'Here,' Claude said when they had the front office to themselves again, 'what was all that about?'

'Nothing,' Denzil said, but he was uncomfortable. Claude wouldn't forget today in a hurry, and Olivia must have suspected something, too. She had given him reproachful looks as she and her father went into his office. 'Just a customer, that's all.'

'But she said...' Claude began.

'I know what she said. I told you, it was nothing. Now, I've got work to do if you haven't.' Denzil buried his nose in a ledger and Claude, snubbed for once, went back to his copying.

But it was no good. Denzil couldn't settle

to anything. Sprat's aunt and his Uncle Billy. His head swam. He couldn't take it in. Olivia went out, looking hurt and brave, and then Bullivant came out of his office. 'Mr Vargo!'

Denzil laid down his pen, ran a finger around his collar and went in. Mr Bullivant sat down behind the desk and stared at him over his reading spectacles. 'Well? What have you to say for yourself? It was evident, young man, quite evident, that you had been closeted in the inner office with ... that young person.'

Denzil swallowed. No wonder Olivia had looked wounded. 'Yes, sir. That is...' he corrected himself, 'no, sir.'

'Am I to take it that you have some kind of understanding with that lady?'

Denzil shook his head. 'I'll be frank with you, sir. I thought so at one time.'

'But not now?' Bullivant scowled. 'I hope, Vargo, that you have not disappointed her? In favour of someone else?' Jilted her in favour of Olivia and her money, he meant, clear as daylight. At least Denzil could disabuse him of that.

'Not at all, sir. In fact it was the lady herself who decided it was hopeless. Her family does not approve of mine, or mine of hers.' Bullivant was still frowning, and Denzil added, 'In fact, she is a relation of mine, it appears – a sort of a cousin. We have just discovered it ... through an uncle in Canada. But there is an old quarrel between our families. She has just discovered the cause of it and came to tell me.' That was true, at least, without maligning Sprat.

'I see.' Bullivant's face cleared. 'A cousin. That does put rather a different complexion on it. But understand one thing. My daughter is very attached to you, Mr Vargo. Indeed, I understand that there have been – intimacies between you.'

Denzil blushed. So Olivia had told her father about the hand-holding.

Bullivant nodded. 'Well, understand this, Mr Vargo, I cannot stand by and allow her to be hurt. If you have no serious intentions towards her, please do not encourage her affections.'

Denzil said, with sincerity, 'I have no intention, sir, of doing any such thing. I have the highest regard for Miss Bullivant.'

Bullivant took off his spectacles and regarded him benevolently. 'Yes, perhaps you do. Well, you have been frank with me – I will do the same. I have the highest regard for *you*, Mr Vargo. But, as I have explained to Olivia, matters are not altogether straightforward. There is the question of your family. You say that the other young lady's family opposed any match between you; and you can hardly expect us to do less. Your father, so I understand, is not only a mine labourer but a heavy drinker too. You can hardly think that Mrs Bullivant and I would welcome that?'

Denzil gulped and said nothing. Father again. Would he never be free from the man's influence? 'There's no shame in being a miner, Mr Bullivant, but as to the drink.... He's my father and I shouldn't speak ill of him, but sometimes I aren't proud of him myself.'

Bullivant smiled. 'Well, I must not be grudging. My own father came from humble beginnings. You have begun well here, Denzil. You have prospects in this company, I tell you that plainly. But, young man, I must not raise false hopes, either in you or in my daughter. I cannot consent to your marrying Olivia, not at this time.'

Denzil had not expected this. 'Of course, Mr Bullivant. I couldn't expect...'

Bullivant held up his hand. 'No, Mr Vargo, I wouldn't go as far as that. I do not forbid it altogether. In a year or two it's possible that I might reconsider. We shall see. A man must be judged on his own merits. But in the meantime, tread carefully with Olivia. You may continue to escort her – of course – as you have been doing. But do not lead her to hope for more, at least until we have spoken again. I should hate to have to break her heart.' He smiled. 'I will explain to her that it was your cousin who visited.'

Denzil went back to his desk in a daze. He had gone in expecting a wigging and he had emerged having half declared for Olivia.

Perhaps it was the best solution. Olivia was a nice girl and she adored him. Clearly, if Sprat was right, things were even more hopeless in that direction than he had thought. If it wasn't Billy, she had said, it was his father. Dear heaven – supposing that were true!

He told himself he couldn't believe it, but of course he could. With a bit of drink inside him, Father was capable of anything – forcing himself on Billy's girl, for instance, and then threatening her into keeping her mouth shut. Denzil shuddered. If that was the way of it, the whole sorry story would make sense.

Well, there was only one way to find out. One of these fine days, he would go to Penvarris and have it out with his father.

Two

'Another whisky, James? Just a small one, before you go?'

James made a show of demurring, on the grounds of his health, but another little spot of whisky wouldn't hurt him, surely? Damned fine whisky, too. In fact, it had been a most agreeable occasion. Comfortable house, excellent lunch, good library, pleasant grounds. Obviously the Selwoods didn't stint themselves. 'Well, perhaps, under the circumstances. To celebrate my first outing? A very small one then, thank you.'

He allowed the servant to refill his glass, then lifted it up and viewed the liquor judiciously. 'Fine dram, this. You must have found a first-class supplier, Selwood.'

'Shipped down direct from a man in Scotland,' Selwood replied. 'Bullivant's see to it for me. I'll let you have the name of the fellow sometime – he'll get some sent down for you too, if you like. A little pricier than the average, but worth every penny, in my view.' He raised his own glass.

190

'Most kind,' James said, swallowing a mouthful hastily. 'But you see how it is. Not in my own house, that sort of thing.'

Selwood nodded sympathetically. 'But I'm sure Violet...'

'Not sure how much longer I shall be staying,' James added. Dammit, couldn't the fellow let the subject drop? The plain fact of the matter was that James had scarcely the money to send out for a bottle of whisky just now, let alone shipping cases of the finest malt. Left to himself, he thought sourly, he might have managed something, but there was no chance of that with Aunt Jane's solicitor looking into his affairs. He said quickly, to change the subject, 'Dashed fine set-up you've got here, Selwood.'

Selwoon preened. 'Yes, yes. Can't complain. Invested in a little motor-garage business with my son-in-law, and it is working out very well. You ought to think of getting into something similar yourself, my dear fellow. These automotive engines are the coming thing, and there's plenty of opportunity down here. Better for your health than smoggy London. And property is very reasonable here. Why, for a few hundred pounds...'

And James was obliged to listen to glowing descriptions of all the sensible things that he could do with his money, if only he had any. It was discommoding. Here was Selwood, prosperous and contented, with a wife and family, surrounded by everything that a man could desire, while he, James, had nothing to look forward to but failing health and an old age dependent on his Aunt Jane's charity. He began to feel suddenly that the afternoon had been too much for him.

'My dear fellow,' Selwood said, 'how thoughtless of me, taxing you with finance when you are scarcely on your feet. Let's talk of other things. Looking after you, are they, down at Fairviews?'

James muttered something about having brought Fitch with him.

'Sensible fellow. Though a pretty little housemaid you've got down there, I notice. That the one you ran uphill to save?' He gave a snort of laughter.

This was better – the sort of man-to-man conversation James had been missing. 'And all I got as a reward was the company of Nurse Bloom!' he said with mock chagrin, 'though I'd rather have that girl to massage my legs for me.'

That made Selwood laugh again. It made James feel man-of-the-world again. Although in fact his attempts to flirt with the housemaid – Nicholls or whatever she was called – had not been altogether successful.

'You'd be lucky,' Selwood said. 'Girl's

afraid of her own shadow. I tried to have a word to her at that evening of yours, just to put her at her ease, but she looked at me as if I was trying to bite her. Where did you find her, anyway? Not local, is she?'

'You old devil, Selwood.' James was emboldened by the whisky. 'All this interest in pretty girls. You keep your eyes to yourself. And speaking of pretty young women, that's a good-looking filly you had serving at table at luncheon, yourself.'

For a moment he was afraid he had gone too far. But Selwood wasn't offended, and they talked about the relative merits of housemaids until Fitch arrived to take him home in a cab.

The day of the great launch arrived. Tom, who by now was sincerely wishing that he had never volunteered to attend, had been hoping it might rain or blow a gale, so that he would have a decent excuse not to go, but the day was bright and clear. Not, he supposed, that Pincher Nicholls would be deterred by the weather.

Tom was already apprehensive as he pedalled out to the Cove. Pincher had been muttering about using 'log rollers' to get the boat from the yard. It sounded jolly hard work, and although Tom had taken Sprat's advice and come prepared in old clothes and stout boots, he was more than a little relieved to find that the boat was already on the beach when he arrived, chocked up with supports with the water lapping around it.

He had envisaged his presence, somehow, as a small but vital link in proceedings, holding a rope here or directing operations there, but the entire Cove seemed to be involved already. Men were setting out fenders against the wall, and doing elaborate things with ropes and bollards. Others were down on the beach with Pincher, close to the boat, staring out to sea with gloomy expressions. Sprat was there too. Tom sighed. He would have to pick his way out over the seaweed and shingle.

As he paused a woman detached herself from the gaggle of wives who had come out to stare, and came hurrying over. He recognised the person who had come into the shop.

'Hello,' she said. 'You're the fellow from White's! Come to see Sprat, have you?'

There was no point in denying it. Tom nodded.

'Glad of that, if only for her Ma's sake. Seeing too much of that Vargo from up over, she was. Wouldn't be told. Worried her ma to death. Well, there she is – down there with her Pa. See?'

'Thank you.' Tom made to move – even the seaweedy stones were better than this –

but the woman was not to be quelled.

'Course, you knew Vargo, didn't you? Well I hope that Miss Bullivant knows what she's getting into. Turning out just like his Pa, he is, by all accounts. Too free with his fists by half.'

Tom stopped. This was too good to miss. 'Really?'

She made a tutting noise. 'Ooh, yes. Came to blows, and he laid his father out with a skillet. Coronation night, I believe it was. Stan Vargo had to defend hisself with a chair. Mind, he gave Denzil something to think about, too – blacked his eye and all sorts. Boy had to leave home, and hasn't been back.'

Little mechanical wheels were turning in Tom's head. Coronation night! It all fitted. He was right! Mr Holier-than-thou Vargo had not damaged his face by being heroic. It was a common fist-fight. And with his father, too. What would Olivia say to that? He smiled grimly. Revenge was going to be sweet.

'You're sure of that? I heard it was a runaway horse.'

She stared at him. 'Runaway horse? Never was! Thing like that would be round the village in no time. No, he attacked his Pa, that's what.' She seemed to sense his interest, because she began to back-track hastily. 'Or at least that's what Stan Vargo's been telling everybody up the Cornish Arms for months. Course, there's only his word for it, and Stan Vargo couldn't tell a lump of coal from a lighthouse when he's got a few pints in him.'

So the father was a drunkard too. Better and better.

Tom might have asked more, but a voice at his shoulder suddenly said, 'Afternoon, Mr Courtney. Handsome, isn't she?'

Mr Zackary! Tom was so startled that he couldn't make sense of the question, but then he said, 'Oh, the boat you mean! Yes, yes, very nice.'

In truth, it looked to Tom very much like any other boat, although with the new paint and the name *Penvarris Star* in bold letters on the stern it did look smart. Hard to believe that anyone could build it with their own hands.

'Taken a long time,' Zackary said, 'but we finished her in the end, thanks to Bullivant's.'

Tom was alarmed that the conversation might turn uncomfortably to 'priority payments' and he said hastily, 'Well, let's go down and take a closer look, shall we, Mr Zackary?' And down they went, squelching through damp mud and over slimy pebbles.

'Afternoon, Mr Nicholls,' Tom ventured when they got there. 'Nice day for it.'

Pincher was still scanning the sea. 'Aren't so sure,' he said gloomily. 'Weather's all wrong. Only an hour to full-tide, and look at it. Wondering if we shall have the water to lift her. We've put out a kedge anchor so we can try moving her on that, but we might have to give her a tow with the engine-boat yet.'

'Couldn't you do it next week?' Tom suggested.

Pincher withered him with a look. 'Supposed to be highest tide today. We'll have to get her off somehow. No good waiting for next springs.'

'You mean you might have to wait till next year?' Tom was appalled.

Pincher looked at him, and then burst out laughing. 'Don't they teach you anything, gig-racing? Spring-tide's just the highest tide – we have one every month. Wait until next year!' He turned to the man beside him. 'Here, Half-a-leg, did you hear that?'

Tom felt himself turn a dull brick-red, and even the appearance of Sprat, who had been admiring the boat with Zackary, did nothing to improve his mood.

'Pa's worried about the tide,' she said.

'I know.' And he said nothing else, just stood and watched the water coming in as if he too were trying to gauge its depth.

It did come in, further around the boat, slowly at first and then deeper and deeper.

Pa and one or two others waded in up to their knees and climbed aboard. Tom, not to be outdone, slipped off his boots and socks, rolled up his trouser-legs and tried to follow, but the water was lapping the cloth. He scrambled back up to the beach and waited. And waited.

'She's lifting at the front,' Pa shouted from the deck. 'Get the weight forward and let's try that anchor.' Men began straining at the windlass. The chocks had been removed by this time, and the *Penvarris Star* was thumping slightly with every wave, and then settling back again on her rear end. Tom had imagined pushing her at the back, but the water was too deep.

'We aren't going to make it, Pincher,' one of the men called. 'Tide'll be on the turn soon.'

'*Ocean Spray's* standing ready,' Pincher returned. 'We'll try towing her off. Sprat, bring round the pram dinghy. You can row me out to *Spray*. We'll use the anchor rope and I'll try pulling her off with the engine. Tom Courtney'll help you.'

Tom stood aghast. He had no idea what a 'pram' dinghy was, unless it was something to wheel babies in. He watched helplessly as half a dozen men dragged a small, fat rowing-boat down to the water and then passed a pair of oars to Sprat, who had already leapt aboard. The men pushed the rowing-boat deeper, and turned to Tom.

He stared back. 'But...'

'Oh, for Pete's sake, come on,' Sprat shouted. 'We haven't got all day.'

' 'Fraid of getting his trousers wet,' one of the men jeered, and there was a general laugh.

That did it. Trousers or no trousers, he waded out, slipping on the dangerous stones, and seized the side of the dinghy.

'Get in!' Sprat hissed, but he didn't know how, and almost overturned them both before one of the men waded after them and hoisted Tom unceremoniously aboard.

Tom sat there clutching the sides while Sprat took the oars and began pulling strongly round to the front of the grounded boat.

'Mind out,' she said, and Tom ducked as Pincher Nicholls vaulted over the side and dropped into the rowing-boat, making it rock wildly. Tom clutched the sides again.

'Move over.' Sprat inched beside him and Pincher took the oars, rowing away with a strength and speed that left Tom astonished. Out they went to a battered old engine-boat. In two minutes Pa was aboard and tinkering with the engine.

'Let's have that anchor, then,' he said. Sprat rowed over to the anchor rope.

'Right,' she said to Tom, 'you kneel in the back of the dinghy and haul in. I'll row as you go.'

Tom – who had been clinging on for dear life – looked round helplessly. Everyone was watching him.

'Go on!' Sprat said, and he had to let go and turn around. He managed to do it second go, and laid hold of the rope. It was slack, so there was no strain on it, but it was damnably heavy. And cold. And wet. And slippery. He hauled it in, panting and sweating – with fear as much as effort – and the rope did come up, slowly. He took some of the weight over the edge of dinghy, which was now riding dangerously low in the water.

'Come on, lad,' Pincher hollered. 'We'll have the tide turning. Anchor's only lying, it hasn't bitten in,' and Tom quickened his efforts. It was a mistake. He had almost reached the end by now, and the rope had turned to chain. The cold metal slipped though his wet fingers and the anchor snaked into the water again, with a splash which drenched him from head to foot. He heard the roar of laughter from the shore, and Pa's muttered imprecations, and his ears burned. There was nothing for it but to set to and pull again with more determination, and at last the anchor was there, safely aboard. Tom turned around and sat down, trembling.

But it was not over. Sprat sculled over to

Spray, which was inching towards them, and Tom had to let go again to hand up the anchor. Pa, with a snort of annoyance, made it fast to something on the rear deck, and turned the engine-boat half around so he was pointing out to sea. There was a moment's pause, the rowing-boat rocking in his wake.

'Now!' Pa said, and there was a growl from the engine. The *Penvarris Star* sighed, lifted, lunged and floated free. The tow-line tightened and she followed like a feather, suddenly weightless in her proper element. The watchers on the wall clapped and cheered.

Tom expected some congratulations for his efforts, but there were none.

Pa hollered, 'I'll bring her over to the wall. Sprat, you nudge her bows round. We'll warp her in.' The engine-boat seemed to pass within feet of them, and Tom was obliged to cling on again as Sprat rowed right up against the front of the new boat and nudged it towards the wall with the dingy.

Mr Zackary on the *Star* had already thrown other lines ashore, and men were heaving at them, pulling the *Star* alongside. Pa tied up the engine-boat further along and came back to add his weight. It seemed to take for ever, while the watchers in the rowing-boat bobbed on the tide.

At last the *Star* was in position, secured safely alongside, against the fenders. Pa shouted, 'Handsome!' and that was that.

Sprat sat back in the boat, shipping the oars. 'Whew!' She flashed Tom a smile. 'We did it! Well, let's go and lend a hand, shall we?'

Tom thought they had lent a hand enough, but before he could protest she had rowed over behind the other boats and tied up. She reached out a hand and caught a ladder, lashed crookedly against the wall. Only two or three rungs were out of the water and it looked treacherous and rickety.

'Coming?'

Tom looked at the ladder, and at Sprat who was already half-way up it. The rowing-boat was dancing and he knew his legs wouldn't carry him. He shook his head.

'Oh, good idea. You take the boat back. Thanks.' Sprat undid the painter from where she had tied it and tossed it down beside him.

Tom found himself trembling. He was all alone in a horrible little boat with no way of getting out of it except up a rickety ladder tied vertically to a wall. Not even that, he realised with a start. The boat was floating away from the side.

'Hurry up!' Sprat called. 'Tide's going out. You'll be half-way to the Scillies in a minute. Come on. Can't be that different from a gig-boat.'

There was nothing for it. Tom shuffled gingerly to the seat where Sprat had been sitting and lowered the oars. They were unexpectedly heavy. He gave an exploratory pull.

The boat moved. Not much, but it moved. After all, Tom thought, it couldn't be all that difficult. A girl could do it. He pulled again, more confidently this time. No it wasn't as difficult as all that. He looked at the wall. No one was paying any attention to him; they were all busy with *Penvarris Star*. He dug the oars in again.

It took him a long time to get ashore. A little while to work out how to avoid going in circles, good progress for a while, and then another period when he realised that the tide was running more strongly against him and he seemed to be getting nowhere. In the end he dipped an oar over the side and, finding solid ground, simply clambered out, up to his knees, and waded ashore towing the dinghy after him. Even then his ignominy was not over. His boots and socks, which he had left on the tideline, were soaked – fetched up against a stone – and he realised he had been lucky not to lose them altogether.

He looked back to the harbour. They were still fussing about on that stupid boat, putting up rigging and Lord knew what. Tom put on his sodden footwear, and – not even pausing to say goodbye – climbed on his bicycle and squelched away.

Sprat did not even see him go.

Three

It was a week or two before Sprat was in the town again, with another letter to deliver to the Women's Movement. Miss Raeburn had seen in the London paper that her friend, Mrs Pethick Lawrence, had been arrested and was being force-fed in prison. She was sending yet another handsome cheque to help the movement's funds.

Sprat had called at the little house in the alley several times by now, but she was still uneasy about doing it. The tangled weeds, the scrawny cats and the piles of untidy papers seemed to multiply with every visit, and the woman with the curls and the ink-smudges unnerved her – swooping on her the instant she arrived with urgent invitations to attend meetings or read pamphlets. Sprat was always glad to get away before she found herself pressurised into signing something.

However, once again this afternoon she had managed to escape without having agreed to do anything more than take away a handful of leaflets. It was with a feeling of some relief that she hurried across to Causewayhead in the hope of catching the chemist before the horse-bus left. Drat those women, they had kept her there for ages while they jawed on about the 'barbarous treatment of our leaders'.

It probably was horrible, she thought, remembering Megan. Worse than those women knew, gabbling on about women being knelt on while a tube was forced down their throat. It was just an idea to them, like something in a book. She thought of Megan's stricken face. Enough to make your stomach turn.

But it wasn't going to help the prisoners, Megan or anyone else, if she missed the last bus and had to walk all the way home.

The quickest way was up a narrow lane at the back of the houses and the dentist's rooms, and she hurried along it, her mind on Miss Raeburn's lavender soap and tooth-powder. She was so preoccupied that she didn't notice the carriage at the corner, and when a man's voice hailed her it took her a moment to realise that he was really speaking to her.

'Hey, you. Young lady. What's-your-name!'

Sprat looked up, startled. A stout, be-whiskered man of middle years was sitting in the carriage. The driver had clearly gone inside for a moment on some errand, and the man was there alone. He was sitting with the carriage door open, clearly looking in her direction.

'Yes, you!' It seemed to be her afternoon for disquieting encounters. It was that Major Selwood who had come to the Christmas evening and had looked at her in such a funny way. 'Aren't you the girl who works for Mrs Meacham?'

'Yes, sir.'

He was looking at her in the same way now, his face flushed and his breath coming heavily.

'Well, come here, girl. I want to talk to you.'

Sprat glanced up and down the lane but the street was deserted. She didn't like this at all. Yet this was an acquaintance of her mistress. She stepped towards him, the smallest step she dared.

'Nicholls, you say your name is?' Selwood demanded.

'Yes, sir.' There was someone coming. A female – thank heaven for that. 'Wilhemina Nicholls, I am, from the Cove.'

The flush that mottled his face grew a little deeper and more purple. His eyes seemed to bore into her. He said sharply, 'Wilhemina? Wilhemina, you say?'

'Yes, sir.' She edged away.

He leaned out of the carriage, and to her horror he seized her by the arm. 'Let me look at you.'

It would be hard for him to look any harder, Sprat thought. She tried to pull away, but he held her fast. 'How old are you?'

She had half heard about men like this. Men who forced their attentions on you, or – if you struggled – could lose a girl her place by a wrong word to her employer. What could she do? No one would believe her version of events.

She looked down the road again and her heart sank. The woman – it was Miss Bullivant – was turning away, into another street. There was no sign of the carriage driver. In a moment Sprat would be alone.

She wrenched herself free. 'Begging your pardon, sir, I'm wanted. Miss Bullivant...' She indicated the departing figure. She did not stop to finish the sentence, but set off at a scamper along the road. When she glanced over her shoulder the Major was still leaning out of the carriage staring after her, and she quickened her pace still further, calling for better effect, 'Miss Bullivant!'

Miss Bullivant heard her. She turned, looking puzzled, and waited for Sprat to join her. At any other moment Sprat would have died of shame, but she was so anxious to escape from the Major's advances that she kept on hurrying, right up to Miss Bullivant's side.

'Why!' Miss Bullivant said, as Sprat approached. 'I thought you were a stranger, but I have seen you once before. It's Denzil's cousin, isn't it?'

Sprat nodded, speechless with haste.

'Is everything all right? You're looking flustered. Did you call to me?'

'It's ... he ... I'm all right now,' Sprat managed, breathlessly. 'The man in that carriage frightened me, that's all. I told him that you wanted me, so I could get away. I'm sorry, Miss Bullivant, could I walk with you? Just till we're out of sight of him?'

Miss Bullivant smiled. 'Of course you may. I am sorry that he has terrified you so.' She looked at Sprat closely. 'Are you quite sure you're recovered? You look to me as if you need to sit down for a moment – have a cup of tea, perhaps. Step into Bullivant's a moment. My father is not there at present, but something could be arranged for you, I'm sure.'

Bullivant's! Sprat was not at all sure that she wanted to go in there, at least not in this company, but Miss Bullivant had taken her arm protectively and it would have been impolite to refuse. She heard herself say, 'Thank you,' meekly and she allowed her companion to steer her up the steps.

Denzil was there, looking the same as ever. Sprat met his eyes for an embarrassed moment, and then Miss Bullivant was sweeping into action.

'Denzil, my dear,' ('My dear!' Sprat thought, in anguish), 'I ran into your poor cousin in the street. She has had rather an unpleasant shock. A man in a carriage – rather too forward with his attentions. Could we produce a chair for her, and tea?'

Sprat was already feeling shaken, and the way Miss Bullivant said 'we' winded her altogether. She collapsed into the chair that Denzil had produced, and sat there staring at her knees while Claude was sent out to make a cup of tea.

'Do you have sugar anywhere, Denzil?' Miss Bullivant's voice was muted with concern. 'I think the poor child should have some – it is said to be a restorative for shock.'

'Yes, yes, a good idea, Olivia.' Denzil was squatting on his haunches at the side of the chair, looking anxiously up into her face, but Sprat could not meet his eyes again. Miss Bullivant was 'Olivia' to him – of course she was. When you were there to witness it, the closeness between them seemed more real.

'Where do you keep it, Denzil? I'll make sure Claude puts some in her tea.'

'In the cupboard,' Denzil said, without moving his head. 'Thank you, Olivia.'

He said it with such warmth that the simple thanks sounded like an endearment,

Sprat thought miserably. She heard Miss Bullivant's footsteps leave the room.

'Sprat,' Denzil whispered urgently. 'What happened, Sprat? Who was it? That scoundrel Courtney? I know he's been hanging round you lately. If it is, I'll punch his teeth in for him.'

Sprat raised her head wearily. 'Oh, Denzil, don't. You sound just like your father.' The remark was born of misery, but she saw Denzil flinch. 'And no, it wasn't Tom. He did come down to see the new boat launched, but I haven't set eyes on him since.'

'He came to that?' Denzil's sharpness piqued her.

'Talking to Norah Roberts about you, he was, and the tale about the horse. Anyway, why shouldn't Tom Courtney come courting if he likes? Isn't as if there could be anyone else in my life, is there?'

Denzil looked stricken, and Sprat regretted her words. If Denzil was like his father, she thought, *she* was beginning to sound the same as Ma. She softened her tone. 'Anyway, this wasn't Tom. It was that Major Selwood, friend of Mr Raeburn's. I've seen him at Fairviews and he was just the same then – staring at me, and asking questions, and getting hold of me, like as if I was ... I don't know ... one of his housemaids. Or worse. And in the street as well! Frightened me to death.'

She broke off hurriedly as Miss Bullivant and Claude came back with the tea. It was hot and sweet, and she was glad of it. She gulped it down, and – feeling a bit restored, as Miss Bullivant had said – wanted to hurry off.

'I'll have to hurry,' she said anxiously, 'else I won't catch the bus.'

'Well, we can't have you walking on your own,' Miss Bullivant said.

'Claude can walk with you, and make sure you're all right. I would accompany you myself, but we are going out this evening. It's the spring concert, you remember, Denzil?'

So Sprat was obliged to go and catch the bus and leave Denzil to his 'Olivia'. She did not even have the toothpowder or the lavender soap.

Tom was cursing his own impetuousness. Weeks of careful cultivation of old man Nicholls, and he had undone it all in two minutes by bicycling off in a huff. Just because he had got his feet wet and made himself look ridiculous. Heaven knew how long it would take to reinstate himself.

He almost persuaded himself, over the next week or two, that it was not worth the effort. The little milliner sought his company willingly, without his having to work for it at all. In fact, she was more than willing. When he offered to kiss and fondle her of an evening, she was positively eager, and even when, in a darkened doorway, he fumblingly pushed things much, much further she was surprisingly compliant. Tom's image of himself as no end of a ladies' man received a decided boost. And he didn't have to ride miles to do it, either.

But he did go back to the Cove at last. Perhaps his other conquest was just too easy, or perhaps it was the delivery boy smirking, 'How's your heiress?' every morning without fail.

The prospect of Sprat's money was an increasing lure. He had become used to a certain financial freedom at Bullivant's and he wasn't earning the same money at White's, by a long way. There were no premium payments to pocket either, and frankly he was finding it hard to make ends meet. Even little milliners required a certain investment, in the form of penny ice-creams and sherbet fountains.

So a fine Sunday afternoon in April saw him pedalling back to the Cove, ready to offer a hundred excuses to Sprat and spend an excruciating afternoon listening to Pincher Nicholls reliving the boat-launch.

He was surprised when he got there, however, to find that Sprat was nowhere in evidence, although her mother – still looking as pale and fragile as a china doll –

seemed to be up and about again and was sitting by the front door, knitting in the sun. She looked up when she saw Tom.

'Hello, young Tom. Fancy seeing you. Pa was only saying, we hadn't seen hair nor hide of you since he launched the boat.'

'I'm sorry I didn't manage to take my leave...' Tom began.

'Oh, I shouldn't worry about that. I know what Pincher's like. Gets so rapt in the boat that you could shout goodbye until you're blue in the face and he'd never pay any attention. Says you lent a hand when you were there.'

Tom relaxed. Doubtless there had been laughter at his expense, but he hadn't done so badly, he told himself. He had succeeded with the anchor, in the end, and he had managed to get himself ashore with the oars. 'I did my best,' he said with modest pride.

The woman nodded. 'That's what I said to Pincher, though he was fit to be tied when he found out. However did you come to leave the dinghy like that – lying about on the waterline for the tide to reach her? And without even making her fast? Damn near lost her altogether. One of the oars was gone, as it was, before Half-a-leg saw her floating about and managed to wade out and bring her back.'

Tom shut his eyes in horror. It had simply

never occurred to him. He had beached the dinghy high and dry when the tide was going out. He never gave a thought to where the water would be when it came in again. He must have looked a proper fool. He said, to cover his embarrassment, 'Sprat not here?'

Her mother's lips tightened in annoyance. 'No. Got herself in trouble with Mrs Meacham, staying out late in town. Some story about a fellow in a carriage. They were furious with her, and she hasn't had more than an hour or two to come home since.' She looked at Tom. 'Fellow in a carriage, indeed. She was out with that Denzil boy, according to Norah – saw her coming out of his office. As if she didn't know enough to keep away from a Vargo. I don't know. I despair sometimes. Why she can't settle down with a nice steady boy like you?'

Tom saw a chance. 'You think Pincher would consent?'

She looked at him. 'He might well do – though I shouldn't ask him now. Furious, he was, about the dinghy. If I were you I'd wait a week or two, till Zackary pays him the rest of the money for the boat. Things'll be a sight easier then for all of us.'

Tom made a sympathetic face. 'It must have been hard, with doctor's bills and everything.'

The tired face softened. 'That was our

Sprat, that was. She's a good girl really, till it comes to Denzil Vargo. Paid for that herself, out of the money that was left her – and bought me a nightdress too. Got that from you, she told me, so you'll know all about it. Course, when Pincher gets paid, we'll see she gets it back. Can't have the girl going short when we've got money of our own.'

Tom's ears pricked up. It was the first time that he had heard the inheritance mentioned by the family. He said, carefully casual, 'Course, there's quite a lot of money isn't there? The house, and everything. I'm sure she wouldn't want you to run yourselves short.'

Ma Nicholls looked up. 'How do you mean, "the house"? What house?'

Tom could feel his mouth turning dry. 'I thought ... I'd heard ... there was a house in Penzance. Left her by her aunt, or something.' She was still staring at him, and he added hastily, 'Course, I may be wrong. Didn't really take any notice.' He got to his feet. Were his cheeks as red as they felt?

Ma said slowly, 'I don't know who told you that. There's a house all right, but it doesn't come to Sprat, it goes to Mr Jamieson's son in America. Sprat's aunt Gypsy was his second wife, see. No, Sprat's inherited some jewellery. Bits of rings and things. It's selling one of them that's paid the doctor.' She smiled. 'Still, there's enough to set her up with a bit of furniture and that, if you do decide to get wed. I hope you aren't disappointed, Mr Courtney. You haven't been courting Sprat on expectations?'

But of course he had. Why else would he have come pedalling all the way out here, listening to Pincher and his boring boats, when he might have been wooing his milliner? But he couldn't say that, naturally.

'Of course not,' he managed, but it was like drawing teeth.

Suddenly he was furiously angry. Not with Sprat so much, nor her horrible vulgar parents, not even with the stupid gossiping woman who had led him astray. Vargo! That was the name that hammered in his brain. It was Vargo's fault that he had ever met the girl; Vargo's fault that he had courted her at all. And now he had come within an ace of offering to marry her.

He wanted to get away: away from this confounded cove with its anchors and dinghies and treacherous tides. He said stiffly, 'Perhaps I'll take your advice, Mrs Nicholls. I'll disappear before Pincher comes back. When he's forgotten about the dinghy, perhaps...'

But he wouldn't be back. He knew it. She knew it. He could see the contempt in her eyes. Damn Vargo.

Vargo, Vargo. Vargo. He stamped on the name as he punched the pedals round, riding home. And that night, under the shelter of the rocks, he pulled the little milliner to him and thrust himself into her – Vargo, Vargo, Vargo – with such intensity that she cried aloud.

Four

Sprat's visit to the office had made Denzil uneasy. He had promised himself for weeks that he would go down and confront his father – get to the bottom of this Billy business – but he kept putting it off. It was too wet, it was too fine, his mother would be home, his father would be out. He wanted to know the truth, and yet he didn't want to.

In the end, about a month after Sprat's visit, he did screw up his courage and make his way home, his heart pounding against his ribs.

The house looked so abandoned when he reached it – the garden neglected, the windows curtainless – that for a moment he wondered if the unthinkable had happened and his parents had left Penvarris altogether. But no, he would have heard. He had paid the rent as usual, and – on closer inspection – there was the veriest wisp of smoke from the chimney.

His rapping at the door brought no response; it seemed everyone was out. But when he tried the latch the door swung

219

open and he found himself once again in the familiar hallway.

At least it *should* have been familiar. There were the stairs, the same brown-painted anaglypta, the same wriggling crack in the wall. But that was where familiarity ended. No potted plant, no hall-stand, no framed text – THE LORD THY GOD SEEST THEE – on the wall.

He peeped into the parlour. It was the same thing there. The two horsehair chairs remained, but everything else – mats, pictures, sideboard, his mother's precious ornaments, even his own school prizes – had gone. Not even a set of fire-irons beside the empty grate. His mother had spoken bitterly of 'chopping up furniture', but he had never for a moment imagined this. And one couldn't burn plant pots and china dogs. What had happened to them? Sold, he guessed. Or pawned.

He went through into the kitchen, and stopped dead. His father was there, sprawled back on one of the remaining chairs, his head against the wall, snoring like the pig he was. Denzil took it all in – the empty shelves, the meagre saucepan of stew on the hearth, the pitiful fire of sticks and newspaper. Suddenly, his blood boiled. His apprehension vanished.

He seized the sleeping man by the shoulders and jerked him upright. 'Here, you, wake up. I want to talk to you.'

The man half opened a bleary eye, and slumped into unconsciousness again.

There was a bowl half full of water on the table. Mother had been soaking something – one of her handkerchiefs. He lifted the cloth with a finger. There were still traces of blood on it, as if someone had used it to staunch a bleeding nose. He saw red, suddenly, and not only the blood. He took the basin and, with one swift movement, flung the contents in his father's face.

That roused him! He sat up, spluttering and swearing, his fists already raised. When his eyes focused and he saw Denzil, his mottled face turned more purple still. 'You, you young varmint. Get out. Out of my house, you hear?' He tried to struggle to his feet.

Denzil never knew where he found the courage to say coolly, 'My house, in fact. I am the one who pays the rent.' His father reared up, furious, and Denzil added, 'Any trouble from you and I'll have you out, out in the gutter where you belong.'

The man subsided, muttering, and Denzil realised for the first time the change in him. The swagger and aggression were still there, but Stan Vargo seemed to have shrunk. He looked frail, the face hollow, a sickly pallor under the swarthy skin. He got up again, fighting, but he was unsteady with drink.

Denzil's push – none too gentle, admittedly – sent him sitting backwards as though he were a mere shell of himself.

'Sit down,' Denzil said. 'We need to talk.'

His father was down but not beaten. 'Got nothing to say to you.'

'Ah, but I think you have. You can tell me, for a start, what it was you said to Sprat Nicholls when you terrified her in the lane.'

'Sprat!' the man sneered. 'What kind of a name is that?'

'Never mind that!' Denzil retorted. 'What did you say, I'm asking.'

His father looked shifty. 'Couldn't tell you if I wanted to. That Crowdie threatened to have the hide of me if I said it again.'

'You'll tell me,' Denzil said, with emphasis, 'or...' He looked around for something to make good his threat, and his eye lit on the poker, where Mother had left it half resting in the fire, under the papers to make a draught. It was hot. He snatched it up, and brandished it. 'Or you'll regret it.'

It was an appalling thing to do, so fearful that it gave him the terrors ever afterwards. Of course, he would never have used the poker – or so he told himself a million times, lying awake at night and reliving the scene. But it had the desired effect.

His father's face turned paler than ever. 'Don't know what all the fuss is about. Never said anything that wasn't true.'

'You called her a bastard.'

'So she is.'

'Your brother Billy's girl.'

'Who told you that? That Gypsy? Well, it isn't true. Billy never touched the woman – it's that what broke his heart so much. Years and years they were walking out – half the world against them – and she wouldn't let him near her. And then this! Billy was beside himself with it. No, it wasn't his. Didn't know whose it was. Billy thought it was me, one time.'

'And was it?'

'Me, touch a Jenkins?' Father's disgust was so complete that even Denzil was convinced.

'Who, then?'

'I dunno. Never did know, or Billy either. Wasn't his, that's all he knew.'

'Gypsy seemed to think so. Wasn't he offered money to marry her?'

Father snorted. 'So what if he was? That only proves it. If it was his child, Billy'd have married her like a shot, money or no money. Betrayed, that's what he was. I told him then, what else d'you expect from a Cover? So there you are, that's what I said to the girl. Now you know. Got what you came for, so are you going to go now and leave me in peace, or are you going to stay here threatening an old man in his own home?'

Denzil put down the poker (which wasn't

very hot, he realised with relief – there wasn't sufficient heat in the fire for that). Then a thought struck him. He whirled round.

'Who offered him money?'

Father looked shifty again. 'Dunno.'

'But you guess,' Denzil said. 'It wasn't Gypsy, was it? She was a maid, in service. Where would she get that kind of money from? I don't suppose we're talking about eightpence, are we?'

Father went on saying nothing.

Denzil put his hand in his pocket, and brought it out, closed. 'I got half a crown here. Two shillings and sixpence. Thirty whole pennies.' He paused. His father was looking at the hand, licking his lips. You could almost see him calculating the beers. 'Half a crown,' Denzil said, 'and it's all yours. All you have to do is tell me what you guess.' He fingered the coin.

'Could be wrong.' Father's voice was a childish whine.

'All the same,' Denzil said.

'Well then.' A pause. 'It was Billy's wife thought of it really. Same thing happened in her household when she was in service herself. Fellow she worked for, down the big house.'

Denzil took a deep breath. It was possible. More than possible. Perhaps, even, it had not been of Gypsy's choosing. Hard for a girl to complain about her employer if he forced himself on her. And an offer of money, to keep it quiet ... Yes, it could be. 'Who was it?'

Father's beery eyes had never left the coin. 'Don't rightly remember. Big house, down in Penzance. Selwyn? Selgood? Some name like that. I told you, I don't remember. None of my business, was it?'

'Selwood,' Denzil said suddenly. 'Major Selwood. Yes, by God, Major *William* Selwood. It all makes sense. Here!' He tossed the coin to his father. 'Drink yourself to death – the sooner the better for all of us.' He reached up and put ten shillings on the shelf. 'And that is for Mother. I shall ask her about it. And if I hear that you have touched one penny of that money, I'll come back and break every bone in your body. As for *this*,' he lifted the damp, bloodstained handkerchief again, 'you lay a finger on my mother again and I'll stop the rent. I'll have you evicted. I mean it. I'll take Mother, and you can go to the workhouse.'

He felt drunk himself, drunk with power and relief. Up the lane, before he had time to think, and in no time at all he was pounding on the back door at Fairviews, his heart thumping so much that what followed seemed like scenes in a magic-lantern show – mostly an unrelated series of startled faces.

A stout cook standing at the door at Fairviews, mouth agape. 'Nicholls? Serious news about her father? Well, you'd better take her with you, poor girl. I'll explain to Mrs Meacham. But don't be long, she'll have to serve at table.'

Sprat, wide-eyed, half running after him as he tugged her arm. 'What is it? What's happened? Aren't we going to the Cove?'

Raised eyebrows and strange looks from passengers as Denzil pushed Sprat, protesting, on to the horse-bus. 'It's no good saying you'll explain later. I'll be late, Denzil, I'm wanted to serve at dinner.'

Then Bert, Daisy's coachman friend, rattling down the street with an empty carriage, stopping to stare as they passed. 'What are you two doing here? You can't go in there, it's a private house. Besides, they're going out and the Major's in a mood already. I turned up a minute early and he's sent me round the block.'

A red-haired maid, opening the door to his knock and looking them up and down in disbelief. 'A message? For the Major? You may leave it with me. He isn't receiving anyone tonight. He wouldn't see you anyway.'

'He'll see me,' Denzil said. 'Tell him I have a message from a Gypsy Jenkins. She used to work at the house. I think he knows the person I mean...'

The servant looked at him uncertainly.

'Ask him,' Denzil said, and they were shown into a room to wait. Sprat was still standing, tongue-tied, so terrified at her predicament that she could not speak or move.

And last of all, Major William Selwood, blustering with astonishment, his fat face purple with outrage. 'What is the meaning of this? How dare you burst in here? I've a mind to have you horse-whi—' He saw Sprat and the colour drained from his cheeks. 'Ah, it is you. I see.' He turned to his man. 'I'd better sort this out, Wilkins. It won't take a moment.'

The servant left, and the door shut discreetly behind him. 'So!' Selwood said. 'You've come here, have you? What is it you want? Money? Well, you won't get a farthing. You can't prove anything. I was foolish enough to make a settlement once, and I shan't do it again. The girl was supposed to go away, get married...'

Denzil heard Sprat's intake of breath. He didn't look at her. Instead he said, 'She did. She kept her part of your sordid bargain. We did not come here for money, we came for information. I think you have given it to us.'

Selwood was breathing hard. 'I admit nothing. Now get out – before I have you thrown out. I've a good mind...'

'I don't think so,' Denzil said. 'I am sure

this is not something that you wish the town to know about. I know a great deal about your household, major.' He reeled off a few names, remembering stories Daisy had told him.

Selwood looked paler and paler. 'So what is it you want?'

'I told you, nothing,' Denzil said, and then had an idea. 'Unless you wish to offer your coachman accommodation. He wants to get married.'

The look of astonishment this time was positively comic.

'In the meantime,' Denzil said, 'I have found out what I wished to know. Come, Sprat – Major Selwood is waiting to go out. Good-evening, sir.' And without waiting for dismissal he walked calmly out.

When they got to the gates Sprat spoke for the first time since they'd reached the house. 'Denzil! What have you done?' She sounded tearful and horrified.

Denzil rounded on her. 'Proved what you would never have believed. *That* is your father, Sprat, not my Uncle Billy. That's where the money came from which Gypsy offered to Billy, but of course she kept her word and never explained where it came from. Pity she didn't – Billy might have forgiven her, if he knew. But she was too afraid of Selwood, of course, and she held her tongue. No wonder he was looking at you so strangely, and asking you those questions. You always said you looked the spit of Gypsy. He must have recognised who you were at once.'

'And you dragged me here, humiliated me, for that? To prove your family's innocence?'

'Of course I didn't.' It was almost their first argument. 'Sprat, don't you understand? You are not my cousin. You're not my sister. You're not related to me at all. My family didn't betray yours, yours didn't even betray mine! Look at the man! You think Gypsy had a choice? Don't you see, Sprat, I can marry you after all. It's all right.'

She looked at him then. 'How can you stand there and say that, Denzil? Your family won't have it. My family won't have it. They'd die, all of them, if they heard about this afternoon. We've made it worse, if anything. How is it all right?'

'We can wait, Sprat. When we are twenty-one we can do what we like.'

'And what do we live on in the meantime? Your precious Olivia won't like it – and then where will your job be? And I'll be lucky to keep mine after this. I'm late for serving at table, and I can't say where I've been. How could I explain this? And what is Selwood going to do? One word from him and I'll be out of there like ninepence. And with Ma so weak as well. Oh, Denzil, what have you done?' She pulled away from him.

'Sprat!' And again, 'Sprat!'

She turned round fiercely, mocking him. 'Sprat, Sprat, Sprat – is that all you can say? Think of yourself, you do, Denzil Vargo, and not a thought in the world for anyone else. You think I'm glad to know what I have learned tonight? That fat man's bastard – my mother forced to put up with him? I'd a thousand times rather it had been your Billy – at least the poor woman was fond of him. No, Denzil, don't try to take my hand – I can't be doing with it. Go away, for pity's sake, before you do any more damage.'

'Damage?'

'Yes, damage. Don't you understand? You've upset Ma, you've upset me, you've made me look small in front of that revolting man, and now you will have upset Mrs Meacham and I'll be lucky if I have a job tomorrow. I call that damage. And what about Olivia Bullivant? Nice girl she is – very kind to me. And kind to you too – so how do you repay it? Get home to her for heaven's sake and try and make someone happy. And tell Bullivant the truth about that horse before Tom Courtney does it for you.'

She turned away furiously and began the long trek home. He tried to run after her, offer to walk with her – pay for a cab even – but she wouldn't have it. Then Crowdie came past in his farm cart, and Denzil had to watch as she flagged him down, got on the front and was jolted away. She didn't give a single backward glance.

Mrs Meacham called for her the minute she got back, and gave her the dressing down of her life.

'This is disgraceful!' Mrs Meacham stormed. 'Disappearing just when dinner is about to be served, with some story about trouble with your father. So Fitch and Florrie have to wait at table, and when I send Mrs Pritchard down for news they haven't seen you in the Cove. Then, when you do deign to come back – hours later – you "cannot say" where you have been.' She paused for breath. 'Well, I know where you were, young lady. Crowdie tells me you were in Penzance, "talking to a young man". And after all the consideration you've been shown over the years. I'm very disappointed in you, Nicholls. I've a good mind to give you your marching orders here and now.'

Sprat, who had been close to tears, took a little comfort from this. People who had a 'good mind' to do things very often didn't. She said, tearfully, 'I'm very sorry, madam. Very sorry indeed. It won't happen again, I promise.'

'You're very right, it won't! I have been too relaxed with you, Nicholls, I can see. It serves me right: it is too long since I engaged young servants. Well, I haven't said this before, but I am saying it now. No followers. Do I make myself clear? I will not have young men calling here for you, or meeting you on the top road while I am paying for your time.'

Sprat felt herself blush. She hadn't supposed that Mrs Meacham knew about that. 'No, madam.'

'Now, you may go to your room and stay there till you're called. And there'll be none of this extra time off that you've been getting, either. Helping your family indeed! No wonder you forgot your shopping when you went to town. Talking to that young man again no doubt?'

That was true, though not the way she meant it. Sprat toyed for a moment with the idea of blurting it all out, telling Mrs Meacham about Major Selwood and the events of the evening. But it was hopeless. For one thing admitting to being a bastard would bring stigma on herself, and for another Selwood would deny everything. Suddenly she felt a great sympathy with Gypsy. This must have been how she had felt when she found herself expecting Selwood's child. No one would have believed her either.

'Well then,' Mrs Meacham said, all her chins wobbling. 'I hope you feel thoroughly ashamed of yourself. If Miss Raeburn had not been rather unwell this evening, and asked for you by name, I declare I should have sent you packing there and then. Now go, and never let me catch you doing anything like this again.'

'No, Mrs Meacham,' said Sprat, and slunk away.

Florrie and Cook were tight-lipped and disapproving. They had had extra duties and were not best pleased at being left to do Sprat's job as well as their own.

She did discover what had happened to Miss Raeburn, however. There had been another argument with James over dinner. She'd mentioned his bills and he'd started on about that Pethick Lawrence woman, and suddenly Miss Raeburn had come over all queer and had to go to bed.

'Wanted you, she did,' Florrie said severely. 'And there was I, serving dinner. If it hadn't been for Fitch, I don't know how I'd have managed. Never thought I'd say this, but I'll miss him, when Mr Raeburn goes. Now, you taking that tray up to Miss Raeburn or what?'

Sprat nodded and went upstairs with the tray.

Miss Raeburn was sitting up again, in her dressing-robe, scribbling a letter at her escritoire. 'So, Nicholls, you are back? Put the tray there.' She looked at Sprat, her eyes feverishly bright. 'I am writing a letter to

Mrs Pethick Lawrence – so ill, poor lady, after her imprisonment, she is going to Canada to recover. I shall want you to post it, first thing in the morning. Very well, you may leave me now. I shan't need you again tonight.'

She turned back to her letter. And that was where Sprat found her in the morning, grey head resting on her arms, the candles burned down, the supper tray untouched. Sometime in the stillness of the night the spirit of Jane Alice Elizabeth Raeburn had ebbed out softly with the tide.

After he had seen Sprat on the cart, Denzil went home. He hoped to slip upstairs unnoticed, but Olivia was waiting for him. She came out of the drawing-room as he passed and greeted him in the hall.

'Good-evening, Denzil.' She gave him one of her adoring smiles. 'I was hoping to see you.'

Poor Olivia. She was so happy to see him. Denzil groaned inwardly. He was still smarting from what Sprat had said. How was he to extricate himself from this? Olivia put out a hand to him, and he drew away.

'Denzil?'

He shook his head. 'I promised your father...'

Her face lit up. 'You have spoken to him about me?'

Oh dear God, she was going to be hurt. Poor Olivia, she didn't deserve this. He said gently, 'Not ... exactly.'

She was still smiling. 'You are hiding things from me. I guessed that you'd done something of the kind. He has been making enquiries about you. He thinks I haven't noticed, but I have.'

Denzil felt himself pale. Making enquiries! That tale of the runaway horse; Sprat had warned him about it. Well, it was his own fault. He shouldn't have told whoppers in the first place. Well, perhaps it was for the best – Bullivant wouldn't want a liar for a son-in-law. But he'd be turned off from his employment, very likely, and then where would he go? It was just what Sprat had said. Oh, dear God, what a mess.

'Denzil, what is it?'

He shook his head. 'There's something I should have told your father.' He turned to her, and this time he did take her hand. 'Olivia, forget me. I come from the wrong background.'

'That doesn't matter. Not to me.'

He tried again. 'There are things you don't know about me. I'm not the man you think I am.'

'Oh yes!' Her eyes adored him. 'Of course you are.'

He sighed. Her trustfulness was terrible. For a moment he was tempted to tell her the whole sorry story. But no – she would only tell her father and somehow contrive to paint him in glowing colours. Better he did it himself.

She squeezed his hand. 'Whatever it is,' she said, 'I'm sure Father will try to understand. For my sake.'

Denzil could bear it no longer. He relinquished her fingers and fled upstairs. Sprat was right. He would have to clear this up once and for all.

He tried to do it first thing Monday morning. As soon as the office was empty he put down his pen and knocked timidly on Mr Bullivant's door.

'Come in!'

Denzil pushed the door open. 'Excuse me, sir. If you have a moment.'

Bullivant was beaming over his reading-spectacles. 'Ah, yes. Come in. I have been rather expecting this. Olivia said you wanted to speak to me. So, what have you to say for yourself?'

Denzil shrugged hopelessly. 'The fact is, sir, I couldn't go on like this. I have meant to talk to you for some time ... I should have done so. Oh dear, I don't know how to put this.'

Bullivant took off his glasses and leaned back in his chair. 'I think, perhaps, I can make a guess. About your prospects, perhaps?'

Denzil scarcely took it in. He took the bull by the horns. 'The plain fact is, sir, I am here on false pretences. That runaway horse – I'm afraid it was a fiction. The truth is, my father came in violently drunk after the coronation. He threatened my mother and I'm afraid I flattened him.'

'Flattened him?'

'He attacked me with a chair. That's what damaged my face. I'm sorry, sir, but that's how it is. I don't know what came over me. I was ashamed, I suppose. Ashamed of myself, and ashamed of him. But there you are. I shall clear my desk immediately, of course, and I will send round for my things. I won't embarrass you any further. Or Miss Olivia either.'

He raised his head. Bullivant avoided his eyes.

Denzil gulped. Well, he had done it now – it couldn't be undone. He went despondently to the door. 'Goodbye, sir. You have been good to me. Thank you. But I couldn't go on as I was, knowing this.' He let himself softly out.

He was closing the door behind him when Bullivant called suddenly, 'Vargo! Wait!' He hesitated, and the voice called again. 'Come back here.'

Denzil obeyed, his heart in his mouth. Now what?

'Close the door.' Bullivant took a deep

breath. 'Now, I can't say I'm not shaken by what you have just told me. I am. Deeply shaken. But it takes courage to do what you have just done, and don't think I don't realise that. As to the incident itself, I can see how it would happen – I believe that I would have defended my mother in the same way. I only wish you'd had the courage to tell me the truth.'

Denzil gaped. He could hardly believe his ears. 'You mean...'

'I mean that I appreciate your honesty, my boy. And my daughter's happiness means a great deal to me. And, frankly, I need you here. There are rumours of shipping strikes again, and the company needs your skills. No, you may stay on, both here and at home. You have confessed, as the Good Book says. I've forgiven other men for worse. You do repent, I take it?'

Denzil said simply, 'I've never been so glad to get anything off my chest in my life. I'm sorry I ever did it. But I thought you would dismiss me when I turned up with a smashed face, and I'd be on the streets. Who would have given me a room, even, looking like that? In fact, if it hadn't been for Olivia...'

'Hmmph,' Bullivant said, and was silent for a moment. 'Yes. Olivia. This whole matter throws into relief what I was saying earlier. Your background, you see. It is not what we would have chosen for Olivia. But you seem to have broken with your family. And I have been making enquiries ... I understand you have been paying your parents' rent, notwithstanding your quarrel. Honour thy father and thy mother. You seem to have done that, in spite of everything.'

Denzil said sheepishly, 'Shall you tell Olivia what I've done?'

This time Bullivant beamed. 'I think perhaps not, don't you, Denzil? You may tell her yourself, later, if you think fit.' He got up and clapped the startled Denzil on the shoulder. 'Well, my boy, since you have been frank with me – and, more especially, since I believe Olivia will never forgive me if I do not – I have made a decision. You have shown yourself honest – a lesser man would have hidden this. So I give my consent. You may ask Olivia for her hand and, I should warn you, I believe she is certain to accept. So, welcome to the family.' He clapped the shoulder again. 'And now, young fellow, I rather think there is work to be done.'

Denzil said, in a kind of dream, 'But ... I ... that is...' He thought of Olivia's good-natured, trusting face and his courage failed him. 'Thank you, sir.'

And, sweating under his collar, he went back to his desk. Dear God, dear God. Now what had he done?

Five

The death of Miss Raeburn chilled the
entire house. She had endeared herself, in
her precise and prickly way, to everyone in
it. Sprat mourned her, Cook wept, Florrie
pulled in her lips, and Mrs Meacham
ordered flowers and black horses and
arranged to have the body sent back to
London, as Miss Raeburn had apparently
wished.

There was a lot of legal paperwork for
that, and Mr Tavy was obliged to call to help
her sort it out. He had been closeted with
Mrs Meacham for some time when Sprat
was suddenly summoned – and not merely
to bring the tea.

'Come in, Nicholls,' Mrs Meacham said.
'This concerns you.'

Sprat edged nervously nearer. She had
never quite forgotten her first meeting with
Tavy, at Gypsy's funeral. He had recognised
her then, and called her 'Wilhemina'. It
seemed suddenly to have a terrible signifi-
cance. Tavy was a solicitor. He probably
acted for Major Selwood. Did he know the

240

truth? Was that why he called her by her name?

He did it again now. 'Wilhemina! It seems that Miss Raeburn has made you a bequest. Not a great deal, but enough to buy you an apprenticeship – as a milliner, she seemed to think you'd like – although the gift comes with certain conditions and you are not obliged to accept it.'

'She left a gift? To me?' Sprat was dumbfounded. 'But surely Mrs Meacham...?'

'Jane has been very good to me,' Mrs Meacham said. 'She has left me her apartment in London. I am considering selling up here, and moving back. Florrie would like it, I know, and of course James will now be returning to his own flat. It would seem, I fear, very quiet here without them.'

Fitch would be delighted, Sprat thought. Especially if Florrie was going to London too. More than once, in recent weeks, Sprat had felt that there was a special warmth between them.

And then it hit her. She was to lose it all. Fairviews, Mrs Meacham, everything she had known. She had lost Denzil, and now she had lost this.

'Of course,' Mrs Meacham said, 'if you would prefer ...? But I shall have Florrie and Nurse Bloom, and I thought, with your mother so frail, you would rather stay here and choose to take the legacy.'

Sprat turned to Tavy. 'There was a condition, you said.'

'Rather an odd one. She requests that you should spend an hour a week assisting the Women's Movement in Penzance.'

Sprat thought of the alley house with its scattered papers and ink and air of febrile activity. She blanched. 'You mean I'd have to be a suffragist? Join in all those protests and sell papers on the street?' In the gutter, in fact. She remembered how Megan had stood on the pavement and been threatened with arrest for obstruction.

Tavy shook his head. 'No, nothing like that. Just to assist the ladies with their office work, addressing envelopes, that sort of thing. It is an unusual condition, but I believe it is enforceable in law. I understand that Miss Raeburn was quite a sympathiser with the movement – at least the non-militant wing.'

Sprat nodded. 'Of course,' she said, 'I should have to find a position.'

Tavy smiled his fleshless smile. 'I believe I may be able to assist you there. A lady of my acquaintance buys her hats from a milliner in town. It seems the woman there has lost her young assistant – the girl got herself into some kind of trouble and tried to drown herself. They rescued her in time but they had to take her to the asylum – tragic business. However, Wilhemina, it may be fortunate for you. The owner of the shop is looking for another girl to train.' He pressed the tips of his bony fingers together and looked at her over them. 'So, you will let me know what you are minded to do?'

Sprat nodded. In fact, there was very little choice. She had Gypsy's thirty pounds, of course, but that would never have been enough to keep her *and* Ma and Pa while she served an apprenticeship, and she had more or less given up the idea. Now, though, the doors were open.

She asked, because she felt she should say something, 'And if I don't?'

'The money will go to one of Mr Raeburn's creditors. She has elected to leave her liquid assets to them, rather than to her nephew directly.'

'I think I will, then,' Sprat said. 'If Mrs Meacham is really leaving here.'

'Then that is settled,' Tavy said. 'None of this will be immediate, of course; the will has to be proved, and the house here sold. But I will be in touch. And there is one other matter. It concerns your own aunt. Perhaps you know that there were certain papers found in the house? Letters from Mr Jamieson to his wife. They were passed to me, after her death of course, and I ascertained what was in them. I felt that the documents should come to you. Permit me to congratulate you on your legacy. Miss

Raeburn must have been fond of you.'

Indeed she must, Sprat thought, walking out of the room in a daze. How quickly and completely one's whole world could change.

Denzil was living in limbo. He planned, first, to go up to Fairviews and explain matters to Sprat. He practised in his imagination all the way to the Cove, pleading with her to wait and to believe in him, and assuring her that, somehow, he would extricate himself from Olivia and everything would be all right. But when he got there it was to be met by a stony-faced Florrie, who said that there was death in the house and wanted to turn him away.

A little persistance brought him a hasty note sent down from Sprat, telling him the same thing, and saying she had been forbidden followers. Their escapade had brought her trouble, she said, and she had meant what she told him. She had a chance to make a new life and so did he. She wished him well. It was signed 'With fond memories, Sprat' – which was his only comfort – and he folded the letter away in a pocket and trudged wearily back to Penzance. He was to look at it many times in the weeks that followed.

If it was impossible to see Sprat, it was only too easy to meet Olivia. She seemed to be waiting for him at every turn, with an air of suppressed expectancy, and her parents too were beginning to look at him each day with politely questioning smiles. He had long ago started to dine with the family, so it was difficult to avoid these unwanted attentions.

Denzil groaned inwardly. He had made no formal declaration to Olivia; in fact he had not mentioned the conversation with her father – hard to explain to a woman that he hadn't meant to offer for her hand. But it was clear that Bullivant had indulged his daughter, once again, by letting her know what had happened. Worse, when they were alone together Bullivant began to mention, apparently casually, a celebrated case of breach of promise which had recently been successfully pursued in the county.

Denzil did not know how to comport himself. He tried for a time to lose himself in work. Heaven knew there was enough to do. The dreadful news of the *Titanic*, growing in horror with every edition of the papers, was of especial concern to Bullivant's – the company had goods in transit in her hold. Then, only days later, the Port of London closed again (they were back on strike, this time demanding a closed shop) and there were another three weeks of frantic activity over more lost and delayed consignments.

But nothing could put it off for ever. It was

Olivia herself who brought things to a head. They had all been to another missionary evening, and she dallied in the hallway to say good-night. Her parents, with indulgent smiles, had made themselves scarce with indecent haste.

'Denzil!' She came towards him, smiling.

'Good-night, Olivia. It has been a pleasant evening.' He turned to go.

'Denzil! Don't turn away from me. Denzil – dearest – I know that you have spoken to Papa and he has given his consent.'

Oh dear heaven, it had come. Denzil turned towards her, his heart in his mouth. 'Olivia, little Olivia. Oh...' He couldn't do it, couldn't wipe that trusting smile from the kind, homely face. He said lamely, 'I can't ... ask you...'

She took his hands in hers. 'Of course you can, you foolish boy.'

He turned his head. He couldn't meet her eyes.

'What it is, Denzil?'

What is it? I love someone else, but she won't even see me. I have held your hand, raised your hopes – raised your father's hopes – returned your kindness by betraying you. You are a dear sweet girl but I do not want to marry you, so go away and break your heart. He couldn't say that. He said miserably, 'If you only knew...'

'It's your family,' she said suddenly. 'That

father of yours, isn't it?'

It was an excuse and he seized it gratefully. He squeezed her hands. 'He's violent, Olivia. A drunkard and a bully. I couldn't ask any girl...' That was true, he thought miserably. Sprat was right. With a father like that, no decent girl would have him. 'I couldn't bring that shame to anyone.'

'Oh, Denzil, is that all it is? But don't you understand, dearest? I learned long ago not to care what the world thinks. If I have you, that is all I ask. Denzil, I have thrown decorum to the winds. I know you would not first have chosen me – my father has told me about your cousin – but I will make you a good wife. I love you. I will make you love me. You like me already, a little. You do like me, don't you?'

He couldn't bear it. He said, 'I like you a great deal. You are a dear sweet girl...' He looked at her, and the 'but' died on his lips.

'Then what are you waiting for? Do you not want to marry me?'

Could he say no? Dear God! 'It would be a great honour, but...'

'Then it is settled. No, dearest, say no more. I know what this has cost you, in pride – confessing your father's weakness – and I love and thank you for it.'

He said helplessly, 'I cannot marry you ... not now.' Visions of breach-of-promise suits floated before his eyes.

'My dear, of course. We can wait. Years if you want. But we must at least tell Papa the good news. I know he has been waiting for it. And – between ourselves, dearest – I know that he has news for you. He plans to install you as manager of the company, before we wed. After all, it will be yours one day. Oh, dearest, I am so happy.'

With the greatest simplicity she lifted up her face to be kissed, and Denzil, with a sinking of his heart, took her in his arms and buried his head in her hair. It was done. To Mother this would seem the summation of a dream.

Poor Sprat. Poor Denzil. Poor, poor Olivia.

Sprat heard the news from Norah Roberts one day when she was on her way down to the Cove to see Ma.

'Afternoon,' Sprat said, very briskly. She had only a half-day off a fortnight and, coming as she now did from Penzance, these afternoons were very precious to her.

But Norah had stopped and put down her basket. 'I see your Denzil Vargo has fallen on his feet then. Engaged to marry Bullivant's daughter, and made up to be a manager too. Trust an up-overer! Fall out of a tenth-storey window, they would, and still land on their feet. Still,' Norah grinned knowingly, 'don't suppose you mind so much these days. Liking your apprenticeship, are you?'

'Hard work,' Sprat said, with feeling. 'But it's interesting.' In fact she was developing quite a skill at it. She was 'living in' over the hat shop in Penzance, taking care to keep out of sight of Denzil, whose offices were distressingly opposite, and learning – with roughened fingers – to wind plaited straw into a child's bonnet. That and, for an hour a week, addressing envelopes down at the alley house. 'I'm learning all sorts...'

'That's nice,' Norah said vaguely. She gave Sprat a nudge. 'How's young Mr Courtney then?'

'Haven't seen him for weeks,' Sprat said briskly. 'Now if you'll excuse me, Ma'll be waiting.' And she hurried off before Norah could say more.

Denzil engaged! She *did* mind. Of course, it was partly her own fault, she knew that – he had wanted to have her and she had sent him away. But she had done the right thing. It was clearly hopeless, now as then. All she could do was wish him happiness.

She walked down to the Row and let herself in. Ma was pleased to see her. Looking frail as ever, but working gallantly. She put down her hearth-brush when Sprat came in and set the kettle on, limping – as she always would.

'Brought you some chicken scraps,' Sprat said, unwrapping them as she spoke.

'That's nice,' Ma said without looking, and Sprat caught her breath. She knew Ma's ways of old.

'What is it?'

Ma sighed. 'Aren't rightly sure, you'll have to see for yourself. From that Tavy fellow, from what I can see. It's up there, behind the clock.'

Sprat fetched it down. It was from Tavy, the collection of papers he had mentioned. She made an excuse to Ma and went outside to read it. Somehow she wanted to be away, quite alone. She walked out on the cliffs, watching the wind fret the grey water, and then at last opened the envelope with trembling hands. 'To be opened in the event of my death'.

It was all there, everything she knew already. A letter from William Selwood, then a subaltern, offering money to wash his hands of the whole affair. A note from Gypsy to James Jamieson, confessing everything – how her employer had made advances, then demands, and how she had been too frightened to refuse. 'I took his money,' she wrote, 'largely in the form of a ring. It belonged to his mother and is worth at least £30. His daughter shall have it, if nothing else, but I have kept the letter too, in case one day my poor child finds herself in want. He would find it hard to deny what he wrote in his own hand. I only regret that

I have caused so much unhappiness, to my family, to Billy Vargo and now to you. By the time you read this I shall be dead. I hope you can all forgive me.'

She stood for a long time staring out on to the sea. She would have to keep Gypsy's letter, at least long enough to show it to Ma. Poor, unhappy Gypsy. But the other letter? She looked at it again. What would Major William Selwood pay to have this back in his possession?

She tore it into tiny pieces and tossed them, like snowflakes, into the rising wind.

When she got back to the house Norah was there. Ma cautioned silence with her eyes, but there was no need for warning.

Sprat spent the rest of the afternoon talking about blocking-felt, and the relative merits of feathers and cherries as trimmings for bonnets. No mention of the letters, or even of the hours she now spent putting suffragist leaflets into envelopes. Though if Norah found out about that, it would give her something to talk about apart from that pesky Tom Courtney. At least, Sprat thought, he seemed to have stopped calling round.

Six

Months passed, and the nets that had closed around Denzil seemed to be drawing tighter. His new responsibilities weighed heavy on his shoulders, both at work – he was 'trainee manager' now, and Bullivant was showing him the ropes, but he'd had no idea how much there was to running a business – and at home.

At Bullivant's home, that is. Denzil had no contact with Penvarris now, beyond occasional news through the Vicar of St Evan. Father, he learned, was 'much the same as ever', which was presumably to say that he was drunk and belligerent, but Mother was well and tearfully grateful for the money he had sent. He sent another contribution and went on paying the rent. Apart from that he tried to forget. Penvarris reminded him of Sprat, and he couldn't bear to think about that.

There was no news from her, none at all. Even Mr Zackary's boat was finished now, and there was nothing to bring her into the office. He had thought he glimpsed her, once, in the milliner's shop opposite – but the girl he'd seen was clearly an apprentice, and of course it couldn't have been Sprat! Not even very similar, probably – it was just that he saw Sprat everywhere.

But he was promised to Olivia now, and there was no honourable way out. It wasn't Olivia's fault, she wasn't silly or vain or mean-tempered – it was just that she wasn't Sprat. But her tender concern for him, her anxiety to please and her worries over his slightest mood were becoming hard to bear. Simply, she loved him too much, and he began to resent his inability to love her in return.

He did the right things. Squired her to concerts and missionary teas, took her walking on the cliffs and riding on the swing-boats at the fair. And she was happy, he was fairly sure she was happy, clinging to his arm and gazing up at him with loving eyes. It was the best that he could do.

The new year had begun well enough – largely due to his new status. For Christmas he had given her a little music box with a wind-up bird that lifted its head and sang, and she was so delighted that she was close to tears. He ate regularly now with the Bullivants and enjoyed the most luxurious food he had ever known. Bullivant had raised his salary by effectively lowering the rent, so he was out of debt with the tallyman too and was even managing to send some money home.

So he was appalled, one March afternoon when he was working at the front desk, to have the office door open and see his father walk in. The man was sober, or almost, and dressed 'for best', in baggy trousers and tight brown coat with a scarf around his neck. Even his worn shoes had been cleaned. He was turning an old felt hat in his hands.

He smiled, rather a nasty, shifty smile. 'Hello, son.' Denzil was so astonished that he could make no reply, and Father went on, 'Well, aren't you going to ask your old father to sit down?'

Denzil ignored this. 'What are you doing here?'

Father leaned forward over the counter. 'Heard you were doing well for yourself. Big office and all. Well, I've come to get a bit of what's owed to me, that's all.'

'Owed to you?' Denzil couldn't believe his ears.

'For all the years I fed and clothed you. Years I worried and scrimped to bring you up. Now you've fallen on your feet. You wouldn't cast me off like an old glove, would you, son?'

'What do you want?' Denzil was uncomfortably aware of Claude, gazing with wide eyes from the inner office. 'Why have you come here, embarrassing me?'

His father's voice took on a whining tone. 'Embarrassing you? When I come to ask you for a few shillings? Isn't too much to ask, is it, you here in luxury and us shivering over a single coal in a grate.'

'I send money to Mother,' Denzil said. 'I shan't give it to you. Coals indeed! I know where you would spend it.' He sighed. 'Does she know you're here?'

There was a sound at the front entrance. Someone was coming. Stan Vargo glanced towards it and raised his voice deliberately. 'Let your mother know I've had to come, cap in hand, to beg a few pennies from my own son? I wouldn't humiliate her. But if you won't help me, you won't. Have to go back, I suppose, and sup on a bit of dry bread while you lord it here.'

'I won't give you money,' Denzil said through gritted teeth. 'I'll find you a job, if you're prepared to work. Supposing you can stay sober long enough.'

It seemed a reasonable solution, but his father sneered. 'A job? Sweeping the yard, or shifting parcels? Your own father, while you swank around in a fancy suit indoors?'

It was, in fact, very much what Denzil had had in mind. He sighed. 'You work, I'll pay. That way you won't be down the Cornish Arms all day. It's the best I can offer.'

For a moment Father looked furious. He

took a step forward. Instinctively Denzil clenched his fists.

A mistake. 'Aren't going to hit me again, are you?' Father wheedled, and Denzil paled as he glimpsed Olivia's startled face in the doorway. He shook his head at her and she tiptoed away, but the damage, Denzil knew, had been done.

He was angry now. 'Get out, do you hear? This is my office and you have no business here. Go on, now – before I call the law on you.'

Father looked threatening, but thought better of it. He began to slink away.

'And don't come back,' Denzil shouted after him, 'unless you think better of it and want an honest job.' It would be tight, with the business as it was, but something could be found. Sweeping the yard, as Father said, or working somewhere the foreman could keep an eye on him.

'My own son,' Father called, for the benefit of Claude. 'Turns me away.' But he went, closing the door behind him.

Claude came out of the inner office, his face a mask of horror.

Denzil forced a smile. 'Take no notice of him. He's a drunkard and a liar – and he'd drink every penny I gave him. He'll be back. Won't be able to resist the offer of a job – even if it does mean working for his son.'

Claude nodded doubtfully, and Denzil

might have said more, but a moment later Olivia came in. She too was looking pale and shaken.

'My father,' Denzil said hopelessly. 'Come to beg money to drink with. You see how it is. I offered him work, and he went away.'

Olivia said, 'Yes,' reproachfully, and changed the subject.

But she remained so disapproving and withdrawn that Denzil was moved to say to her later, as they walked home together in the fading light, 'About my father, Olivia. You don't understand...'

'I understand perfectly. He drinks. But the man is starving, Denzil, lacking even a few coals. He must have been desperate, to come to you.'

'I'll send them money, then, since you wish it,' Denzil said, with a sigh. 'But I shall send it to Mother. At least that way they will eat. I would prefer that he worked for the privilege. Otherwise he will be begging on my doorstep constantly.'

'Well,' Olivia said, sharply, 'I have a conscience, Denzil, if you have none. Your own family, burning furniture for heat and pawning everything they own. Don't look so startled; I was on the step and he told me everything. I had only thirty shillings with me – but I gave him what I had.'

Denzil stared. 'You did *what?*' He took her by the shoulders. 'Dear God, do you know what you've done? He'll drink himself witless on money like that. He'll be in some public house now, laughing at the pair of us, until he's drunk enough to get nasty. Pick a fight, more than like, and Lord knows what he'll do to Mother when he gets home. I'll have to stop him.' He sighed. 'I've missed the horse-bus now and I'll have to walk to Penvarris. Just pray that I'm in time. He's a very devil with drink in him. I wish, just for once, that you had respected my wishes.'

And, leaving the astonished Olivia staring after him, he strode off up the road. He didn't see Tom Courtney approaching on his bicycle.

But Tom Courtney had seen *them*, and he could hardly believe his good fortune. Vargo and Olivia arguing in public! There could be no doubt of it! Vargo had stormed away with a face like thunder, and it almost looked as if he'd given her a push. Wait till Bullivant heard this. That would be something! Tom had waited a long time for his revenge.

Thank heavens he had borrowed the bicycle. He had taken to doing so last year, every time he left the Emporium, in order to avoid walking past the hat shop. He didn't want to meet the little milliner.

There had been a dreadful scene the last time they had met. Back in the summer, that had been. She had thrown herself on him, begging and weeping, and demanding that he marry her. She looked a fright, too, which didn't improve things, and when he tried to decline politely she actually started thumping him. Tried to blame him for the condition she was in. As if it was his fault! He hadn't pursued *her*, quite the contrary. And who was to say that it was his child, more than someone else's? Girl like that, who could possibly be sure?

He had got rid of her in the end. She had gone off, screaming and sobbing and threatening to throw herself under a train, but although he'd had an anxious week or two there had been nothing in the papers: no suicides, no accidental deaths. Nor had she carried out her threat to come and confront him at White's. As the months had passed Tom had begun to breathe more freely, but she must have had the child by now, so she could be out and about again. He borrowed the bicycle every night, just in case.

He pedalled a little harder now, until he came alongside Olivia Bullivant. She was crying.

'Miss Bullivant!' He was off the bicycle in an instant. 'What are you doing here at this hour? It will be getting dark soon. You should not be out alone. Allow me, please, to escort you home.'

She looked at him thankfully. Yes, thankfully. Vargo had certainly blotted his copybook here! Tom swallowed his triumph and said, with concern, 'You are upset. Don't tell me if it distresses you, but if there is anything I can do...' He made a bold decision. 'You know, Miss Bullivant, that I have always held you in the very highest regard and – yes, affection. If I can be of any service, it would be more than an honour. It would be a joy.'

'Thank you, Mr Courtney. It is nothing. Truly nothing. Only that Mr Vargo's father called at the office and I gave him money. Denzil is distressed with me.'

Tom had rehearsed a thousand ways of taking his revenge. He had fantasised about confronting Bullivant, marching into the office and telling him the truth about Vargo – but of course, Bullivant would never have listened. When he first learned the truth about that drunken brawl he had even started composing anonymous letters in his head. But then the little milliner had started making trouble and other things had absorbed him.

And now here was Olivia, offering him the opportunity on a plate. He said, carefully, 'Ah, yes, his father. They never did get on. Has poor Mr Vargo recovered from when Denzil attacked him?'

A hit. A definite hit. Olivia's face paled still further. 'Denzil did that?' She was trembling. 'Mr Vargo said that Denzil hit him, but

I couldn't believe it of him.'

Tom abandoned the bicycle and took her by the arm. It was daring, but she didn't protest. 'I'm afraid it's true, Miss Bullivant. It is the gossip of the village. That story about the runaway horse – it wasn't true. That was a lie he told to explain away his bruises from the fight. His poor father tried to defend himself, but he is an old man. Denzil knocked him unconscious with an iron pan.' He saw her face and said, 'If you doubt me, ask him. He cannot deny it.'

She said, 'Denzil!' with a sob.

'I'm sorry, Miss Bullivant,' Tom said, with a singing heart. 'I'm afraid Denzil is not the man you thought him. I tried to warn your father, once, but in the end my better nature overcame me, and I argued that he should be given another chance. I have regretted it ever since. Denzil had me dismissed, you know that?'

She shook her head.

'Oh yes. This famous priority system he devised – the one your father is so pleased with – well, he didn't devise it. I did. I was trying it – on an experimental level – intending to tell your father when I had it running properly. But Denzil got to hear of it just before I was ready, and presented it as though I was doing something dishonest. Of course, he has your father completely fooled. He won't hear a syllable against him.'

He had gone too far. Olivia said, weakly, 'I don't believe it. I won't hear you speak of my fiancé so.'

He nodded. 'Yes, of course. I should have known that you would defend him. It is noble of you. I only wish that he were worthy of your trust. There was another girl, once...'

She interrupted. 'I know. His cousin. He has been frank with me about that. They were fond of each other, but there was some sort of family feud which made it impossible.'

'That's what he told you?' Tom hadn't heard the 'cousins' story. Perhaps Vargo really *was* more of a scoundrel than he looked.

'He told Father. Why, what is it? Why are you looking at me like that?'

'That isn't his cousin,' Tom said. 'I know the girl's mother and father. They disapprove of Denzil as much as I do.' He saw an opportunity suddenly, and seized it with both hands. 'I don't believe the girl has any cousins. She did have an aunt, who left her some money. There was a rumour of quite an inheritance, but it turned out to be very little. Of course, I am sure that had nothing to do with Denzil abandoning her and turning his attentions to you.'

'Abandoning her?'

'Miss Bullivant, I shouldn't tell you this.

But I have seen the poor girl leave the office in tears, because he would not see her. I felt so sorry for her I walked her to the bus and bought her a penny ice-cream to cheer her up.' He smiled doubtfully. 'It is hardly the weather for ice-cream today, but a pot of tea and a penny bun, perhaps? I can hardly tell you how honoured I should be, and I should hate to deliver you home in this tearful state. Your father would never believe that it was not my doing.'

'Mr Courtney, I couldn't. A young lady and a gentleman to whom she is not engaged.'

But she was wavering, and he pressed his advantage. 'If it were not for Denzil, you know, perhaps ... No, that is too much to hope. But I have never altered in my feelings for you, Miss Bullivant. Never.' He smiled ruefully. 'There was a time, you know, I used to be *invited* to take tea with you.'

She hesitated again. 'Well ... if we are discreet. Certainly, I do not wish to meet Mama with my eyes red and swollen. She would be angry with me for giving a man money for drink, just as Denzil was.' She looked up at him tremulously. 'Said they were starving, poor man, and I believed it.'

Tom pressed her arm with his own. 'You are too trusting, Miss Bullivant. It is a charming fault. And you must not blame yourself, the man may be telling the truth. I have seen the cottage he comes from, and it is pathetic. Does Vargo visit his parents?'

Olivia shook her head. 'I have wondered about that.'

Tom judiciously said nothing, but steered her back along the pavement in the direction of a little tea-shop. She allowed herself to be seated, in a corner away from prying eyes, and when he had ordered tea and buns she burst out again, 'Oh, Mr Courtney...'

'Tom.'

She smile tearfully. '...Tom, I have been so worried lately. He has been, not exactly distant, but ... I don't know. Ever since we were engaged. As if...'

'As if,' Tom supplied, 'he had got what he wanted, and didn't need to bother any more?'

She gazed at him, hollow-eyed. 'You think that?'

'Oh, my poor, poor Olivia.'

She was putty in his hands after that, and, walking home in the gathering dark, she even allowed him to slip a protective arm around her.

'And remember, I am in White's any day if you need me.' He pulled her to him and kissed her, very chastely, on the cheek. 'My poor, lovely Olivia.'

The bicycle was still there when he got back.

PART FOUR

June 1913

One

Father was nowhere to be found. He had been seen, however.

Denzil picked up a trail easily enough, starting at the Cornish Arms, where Father had apparently stayed for more than an hour, drinking himself steadily from joviality to hostility, until at last he went for one of the miners and the publican threw him out. Again.

He had been to the Three Choughs, at St Evan, but after a pint or two the barman refused to serve him there, and after a lot of swearing and thumping he had stumbled away. After that, nothing. They hadn't seen him at St Just, although one man thought he had heard him, singing and cursing, in a gateway beside the Penvarris road.

'Never went too close,' he said. 'If 'twas Stan Vargo, I knew better than go anywhere near un. Proper 'andful he is, when he's 'ad a drop too much.'

So Denzil retraced his steps down the Penvarris road, but there was no sign of Father. There was a place where someone might have vomited, but it was dark by now and it was difficult to be sure.

Mother had no news either. When he knocked at the door, she didn't open it until he called her name and she realised who it was.

'I don't know where he's got to, Denzil. Told me he was going out after a job. But he's been gone hours. If what you say is right, I fear to think what state he'll be in by this time.'

'One pound ten she gave him,' Denzil said. 'He'll bring some of it home, perhaps.'

She shook her head. 'You don't know him, Denzil. Bad to worse it's been these last months. Like as if his pride had gone completely. No, if he's got it, he'll drink it. Like that half-crown you gave him when you came.' She sighed. 'Think he'd be half-way grateful, wouldn't you, but all he could do was curse you up hill and down dale for giving *me* a ten-shilling note.'

'At least you got it,' Denzil said. 'I feared you wouldn't.'

'You frightened him,' Mother said. 'Going on about the workhouse. Though there are times, Denzil, I swear to you I'd a sight rather be up there, on the parish, than be stuck here in this house with him. Leastwise then I wouldn't be in range of his fists. There, I've said it, and may God forgive me.'

Denzil sank into a chair. The workhouse – grim grey walls, grey uniforms, grey food, and never a moment's cheer or privacy from one year's end to the next. She knew it as well as he did. And that seemed a better life, to her. Yet he had thought he was helping her, paying the rent as he did.

He sighed. 'What are we to do?'

She shook her head. 'I don't know. What *is* there to do? He's drinking himself stupid somewhere. He'll sleep it off sooner or later, and in a day or two – whenever he's spent the money – he'll come rolling in here, madder 'n a bull, and we'll start all over again.'

Denzil raised his head. 'No,' he said. 'We won't do that. There's been enough of this. You got somewhere you can go, tonight?'

She stared at him. 'Go?'

'Somewhere you'll be safe from him. At least for tonight. I'll give you some money. Then tomorrow, we'll see. I'll try to make proper arrangements.'

'Next door would have me,' she said. 'But goodness knows what he'd say if he found out.'

'Just see he doesn't find out,' Denzil said. 'He won't know anything when he comes in, anyway. You send word, let me know how things are.'

He watched her to the neighbour's door, and saw her welcomed in. That at least was a load lifted from his mind. He walked down the road again, but there was no sign of Father and in the end he had to give up.

It was very late by the time he returned to Bullivant's. He did not know that Olivia was still awake, weeping into her plaited hair. Nor that, out somewhere on the lonely cliffs, a man was stumbling stupidly to his death.

It was Half-a-leg who found him. He came into Ma's kitchen in the Row, white as a sheet. 'Pincher here?'

Ma shook her head. 'Gone out with Mr Zackary on *Penvarris Star*. Trying for mackerel on the hand-lines.

Here, my dear soul, what is it? You look as if you've seen a ghost.'

Half-a-leg sat down heavily. 'Nearest thing,' he said. 'Went out round the Head this morning, seeing to the pots, and suddenly I saw un. There's a man there, Myrtle – fell off the top of the cliff it looks like. I went in as close as I could, but I couldn't reach him – need to get in at low-tide with a rowing-boat, then maybe you could fetch him out.'

'Dead?'

'Dead twice over, Myrtle my 'andsome – if the fall didn't get him, the sea'd have done.' He had taken the glass of elderflower brandy she had given him and was drinking it like a man starved with thirst. 'Face down in the water he is, on they jagged rocks right under the point. Body looks in a bad way too – though how anybody came to be wandering about right up there close to the edge, I don't know.'

Ma shook her head. 'Can't be anyone from round here. They'd have known different. Always been chancy, that part of the cliff – landslips, rock-falls and all sorts.'

Half-a-leg wiped his mouth on the back of his hand. 'Dunno,' he said. 'Couldn't see his face. 'Less he jumped off a-purpose. Brownish coat on him, that's all I know. Well, if Pincher's not here, I'll have to find someone else to help me. Take two, it will – manoeuvring the boat and ... everything else.' He wouldn't mention the body more than he could help, Ma knew. Like most fishermen he was superstitious. 'Peter Polmean's no good for a job like this, specially now he's got a weak leg. Gibbering, he'd be, and no use to man nor beast. And most of the men are out to their pots. Pity your Sprat isn't here – she's handier than most when it comes to handling an oar.'

'Who says I'm not here?' And there was Sprat in the doorway. 'What you want an oar for anyway?'

Half-a-leg explained again. 'No good till the tide drops, anyhow. Pincher might be back by then. But if not...'

'I'll help,' Sprat said. 'I aren't expected back till tomorrow. No working down the suffragists tonight.'

'How's that, then?' Half-a-leg enquired.

'They want me there tomorrow night instead. Planning a big parade, they are, for next year – all the suffragists in Cornwall are marching from Land's End to London.'

Ma sighed. Telling him all this was as good as telling Norah, but Ma's frantic signals went unheeded. Perhaps Sprat meant to do it. If this parade was supposed to be public, perhaps it was the kind of news you didn't mind everyone knowing.

'Sprat's got to help them down there,' Ma explained. 'Miss Raeburn made it a condition. Thought a lot of our Sprat, she did,' she added with pride. She nodded at Half-a-leg. 'Well, you'd better pop along and tell Norah what you're planning. She'll be chafing, wondering what you're at.'

Half-a-leg got to his feet. 'Yes,' he said. 'Norah'll likely know if there were any strangers hereabouts. Anyone missing, or that. Only – I couldn't face her, first off, tell you the truth. Nag, nag, nag, she'd be, wanting to know every rag and ripple. Needed to calm me nerves first. Thanks for the drink, Myrtle. I'll be back d'rectly.'

Ma hefted the kettle on the fire. Everything was more of an effort, she found, these days. She said, when Half-a-leg had safely gone, 'Think Christmas has come, Norah will, with two pieces of gossip in five minutes!'

Sprat took the teapot from her hand. 'Sit down. You look worn out.'

'Well,' Ma said, reluctantly obeying. 'It's a shock, isn't it? First this body, and then you. Quite enough excitement for one day.'

Sprat turned. 'That's a pity then. 'Cause I got another one. Been meaning to show you this for weeks.' She pulled a letter from her skirts.

Ma stared. 'That's our Gypsy's writing,' she said. 'Know it anywhere. Good scholar, she was, considering. How she found the time to learn I'll never know.' But of course she did know. Time that she herself had spent winkle-picking, and baiting smelly pots. She sighed. 'What does she say, then?'

Sprat read the letter – at least most of it. There was something about 'I took the money...' and then Sprat screwed up the letter suddenly and thrust it into the fire.

'Well,' Ma said at last, 'I never did! And all these years I blamed Billy Vargo. You were right, you see. You said it wasn't him. Wonder why Gypsy never told me?'

'She promised she wouldn't,' Sprat said. 'That's how she took the money.'

'Yes,' Ma said. 'What was all that, the bit you didn't read? I aren't stupid, Sprat. I could see there was more.'

273

Sprat turned away. 'Nothing,' she said. 'Just a private message for me asking can I forgive her.'

Ma shook her head. 'She should have told me,' she said again.

'Meant it for the best,' Sprat said. 'Like you did. We've all got our secrets, haven't we?' She prodded the ashes with a poker, and Ma saw that she was crying. 'Shaken me up, all this talk of corpses. I wish Pa would come back. If I'm to give a hand, I'd like to get it over. Nasty work, it'll be.'

When Denzil came down that morning Olivia was waiting for him, her face grim and ashen.

'Denzil, I must talk to you.'

She was still shaken from his chiding yesterday, Denzil thought. Well, he had meant every word. 'Not now,' he said, matching her tone. 'I am already late – thanks to you. You know my father is still missing? I was out looking for him till the small hours. Still, it should not be long. He will have drunk every penny by now.'

It was cruel, and he saw her flinch. He said, more equably, 'Why don't you come down to office? Your father is going out to a meeting later this morning – if you wish us to be alone. Claude Emms will be here in a moment for the briefcase, and I cannot keep them waiting.'

She nodded, but did not let him pass. 'Denzil, there is one thing...'

'What is it?'

'That accident to your face. Was it a horse?'

He closed his eyes. Dear God, where had she heard that from? And why now, of all times?

He took her gently by the shoulders. 'I am sorry that you have heard it from elsewhere – I had hoped to tell you myself, when we were wed. No, Olivia, it was not a horse – it was an argument with my father, as you have no doubt learned.'

Her lip trembled. 'You lied to me.'

'I lied to you all,' he said. 'And I am heartily sorry. But I did not know you then, Olivia. It was your kindness to me then, your willingness to help a lad in distress, that first made an impression on me.' It was true; why then did he sound and feel so strained, as though it were mere meaningless oratory? He could not meet her eyes.

She must have felt it too. She said, 'You could always charm me with talk, Denzil.'

He looked at her then. 'What is it? What's happened?'

'Nothing has happened, Denzil, except that I have opened my eyes. I don't know why I didn't see before. It is not me you love, Denzil: indeed, sometimes I think that our engagement irks you. If that is so, tell me, and I will release you willingly.'

'Olivia!...' But already there was a tapping at the door, and Daisy was tiptoeing into the hall, briefcase at the ready. Mr Bullivant came down the stairs.

'Ah, there you are, Vargo. Ready to go, are we? Didn't see you at breakfast.'

'No, sir,' Denzil replied. 'I was out very late. I had a problem at home. Someone gave my father money – and you know what that can lead to.' He didn't look at Olivia, but he heard her catch her breath.

Bullivant said, 'Your mother?'

'Safe,' Denzil said.

Bullivant nodded. 'Very well. Time that we were off. I have some papers to look at before that meeting with Selwood this morning. Goodbye, Olivia.'

'I shall drop by later,' she said, and Denzil knew the message was for him. Breakfastless, he set off for work. It was quite like old times, he thought.

It was busy at the office and Denzil was not sorry about that. Clients and papers to keep him occupied. Bullivant's was getting on its feet again and customers were returning. He spent an hour dealing with new orders, and then turned to the paperwork, but it was almost impossible to concentrate.

Olivia, first. What had possessed her to speak to him like that? Because he was brusque with her yesterday? Or, more likely, because she had learned the truth about his injuries – from Father no doubt. Wherever he was.

It was to be hoped he hadn't found his way home and started terrorising Mother. And, with that much drink in him, what sort of guard would he keep on his tongue? Not that people would believe Stan Vargo, of course, but rumours had a way of percolating. And that brought him back to Olivia again.

He was still thinking in circles when there was a timid knock on the front door. He looked up, frowning. Who on earth would knock in that way? People just opened the door and came in, as a rule. The little bell on the doorjamb was sufficient warning of their approach. A gypsy perhaps, selling pegs or heather, or a street musician with a monkey on his arm, wanting a penny to play his hurdy-gurdy somewhere else.

He went out to see.

Mother was there. He was so surprised to see her that he quite forgot to invite her in. 'Mother, what is it? You're shaking, what's the matter?' How pale and ragged she looked, here in the prosperous town.

She shook her head wordlessly.

'Father?'

She shook it again. 'No. Or rather, yes. It could be. Denzil, you'd better come. There's a body, Denzil, fallen over the cliff. They can't get to him yet, because of the tide, but he's wearing a brown coat like your father was. Crowdie heard the news, just this morning, from Norah Roberts down the Cove. It was her husband found it. Crowdie gave me the money for the bus to come and find you.' She gave a shuddering sigh. 'Might be Stan, Denzil, lying there dead and drowned.'

Denzil was trying to take it in. 'Father, drowned?' A wonder hell would have him, he found himself thinking, but he didn't say that aloud.

' 'Tisn't certain, Denzil. There's nobody seen his face.' She was weeping, great helpless tears that coursed down her face. She hardly seemed aware of it. 'Going to row round they are, when the tide eases. Mr Roberts and whoever he can find. Oh, Denzil!'

He reached out to her. 'Mother, don't mourn. You said yourself, it may not be him yet. Time enough for tears after.'

She looked at him, and he knew in that instant what her life with Father had been. 'Denzil, son,' she whispered, 'I aren't crying for fear it's your father lying dead. I'm crying, God forgive me, in case it isn't.' She turned her head away.

'I'm coming, Mother. Let me get my coat.' He went back into the office, setting the bell jangling. 'I've got to go to Penvarris,' he said

278

to the startled Claude. 'There's an emergency. One of my family.' He seized his coat. 'Tell Mr Bullivant I'll be back as soon as possible.'

He rushed back to his mother. 'We'll take a cab,' he said, 'and hang the expense. I want to get there before the tide eases. If anyone is rowing round with Mr Roberts, it's going to be me.'

He had forgotten all about Olivia.

So he was not there when she came to the office, and Claude could only shrug his shoulders and say, 'I don't know. He didn't leave a message. Said it was urgent and rushed off like a train. Went off to Penvarris with her, a woman, I saw them through the window. Something about a relative, that's all I know.'

And by the time Olivia had slammed the door behind her and flounced away, Denzil was half-way to the Cove.

Two

'Of course, madam, if you prefer we have it in the blue,' Tom said, with his most urbane smile. 'It would flatter your eyes.' Silly old trout. She would look ridiculous in either of the blouses.

Still, he seemed to have done the trick. 'Perhaps you are right, Mr Courtney. I'll take the blue.' She hesitated. 'Although ... oh, perhaps I will take them both on approval, and let my husband decide.'

'Very wise, madam,' Tom said, trying not to grit his teeth. 'Miss Edgely, if you could see to Madam?' He had caught sight of Olivia Bullivant, hurrying towards the shop door. He extricated himself from his customer and hastened to meet her.

'Miss Bullivant, can I be of assistance?'

'Tom, I must talk to you.'

That sounded dangerous. He looked around. There mustn't be a scene. There had been enough trouble with the milliner. But this was different. He couldn't just have Olivia ejected – not if he was wise. He thought quickly. She was flushed and evidently distressed.

He took her by the arm, with an air of courteous concern. 'My dear Miss Bullivant, are you not well? Please, take a chair. Miss Edgely, a glass of water for the lady.' He picked up a pair of gloves from the display and fanned her face ostentatiously.

'But...' Olivia began to protest, but he was too quick for her.

'A little fresh air, perhaps? Allow me, Miss Bullivant.' He shepherded her towards the door. The customer with the blouses was offering smelling-salts. He waved them away. 'She will be all right in a minute. Leave her be.'

The woman went, reluctantly, and he turned to Olivia. 'What is it?'

Olivia gulped. It made her look like a frog. She did, though, have the sense to follow his lead and lower her voice so she could not be heard. 'Oh, Tom, it's Denzil. You were right – everything you said. Tom, I have been such a fool.'

This was distinctly promising. But not here, not now. He had to get her away from the shop-girls and the customer, still hovering wide-eyed in the shop. Miss Edgely came waddling out with the water.

'Thank you,' Tom said, without taking it. 'But I think I will escort the lady home. She would be wise to rest, I think. My arm, Miss

Bullivant?' She had the wit to take it without demur, and he found himself escorting her publicly, but perfectly properly, down the street.

'Now then,' he said, when they had rounded a corner and were safely out of view in an alley, 'what is all this about?'

She told him. She was hurt, angry and bewildered. 'And when I confronted him, he promised to see me – asked me to come to the office this morning,' she finished, heatedly, 'But when I arrived, I find that – without notice – he has disappeared to Penvarris with a woman, and left me standing there.'

'That so-called cousin of his,' Tom said, turning the knife. 'My poor Olivia.' He held her at arm's length and looked at her, as if her little rabbit's face was the summit of beauty. 'I blame myself. I should have tried to warn you. But you would not have believed me.'

'No.' She gave him a wan smile. 'I do not want to believe it now.'

It was so easy, Tom thought. Vargo was a fool to himself. All those lies about horses and cousins. And then running off to Penvarris when he should have been at work – chasing after his sot of a father probably, if that gossip woman was to be believed. He said, suddenly, 'There is one way to find out the truth about Vargo.'

She stared.

'The bus goes to Penvarris in a few minutes. We can be on it, if you hurry.'

'But White's...'

'I told them that I was escorting you. Well, so I am.' Anyway, it was half-day closing, so his desertion could only be for an hour at most – and that might easily be covered by Miss Bullivant's 'fainting fit'. He might even be praised for it. He would not have dared suggest the expedition otherwise.

She gave him a reluctant grin. 'It was clever, back there. What you did.'

'Yes,' he said happily. He was rather pleased with it himself. 'But I told you: anything for you. Anything at all.' He held her hands and gazed into her eyes. 'I want you to think of me as your friend. Your very special friend.'

They might be in an alley but they were in broad daylight. All the same she allowed herself to be gathered in his arms. She buried her rabbit's ears against his shoulder.

'Oh, I do, Tom, I do. I do.'

Denzil was only just in time getting to the Cove. Half-a-leg Roberts was already on the beach, tugging a little row-boat to the water. He was assisted by a small, simple-looking lad with a limp, who was clearly more willing than useful.

'All right, Mother, you stay here,' Denzil

said, stripping off his coat and breaking into a run down the path. He was wearing his good clothes but it couldn't be helped. He joined the pair on the beach. 'Pair of hands.'

Half-a-leg looked at him quizzically.

'May be my father round there,' Denzil supplied.

'Row, can you?' Half-a-leg said.

'Should be able to,' Denzil said. 'Had a boat as a boy.'

'Right then,' Half-a-leg said. 'We'll take the gig-boat. Faster by half, and a bit more room aboard-ships. Lucky my cousin left her here.'

'Only two oarsmen?' Denzil said. Usually a gig required four men, three to row and one to cox.

'Got a third one,' Half-a-leg said. 'Here she comes now.' He nodded in the direction of the path.

Denzil could hardly believe his eyes. 'Sprat!'

Half-a-leg nodded. 'Not so good as man, of course, but we aren't looking to row to Scilly. We'll do, the three of us, and Peter can take the bow. Terrify him out of his wits, I 'spect, taking a dead man aboard, but there's no help for it. None of the men'll be in now, with the tide turning, and by the time they do come it'll be too late. Can't leave the poor beggar out there any more'n need be.' They were already dragging the gig

284

down to the water when Sprat joined them.

'Believe it's my father gone over the cliff,' Denzil said, before she could say a word, and she caught his cue and nodded as she took her share of the load.

'Right then,' Half-a-leg said a few moments later, 'in the middle, Sprat. Peter, in the bow – you keep a look-out there. Now then, Denzil, you get in and push off with the oar and I'll give us a shove. Leave the little row-boat where she is for now. Haven't time to put her back – it'll take us half an hour to get round there, with only half a crew. She'll be all right where she is till the tide turns.'

In fact it was nearer an hour – they were pulling against the tide – before they rounded the point. They could see the body clearly now, stranded on the rocks. As they neared, Denzil looked at the coat, and knew.

' 'Tis 'im,' he said. 'I'd know that coat anywhere.' Perhaps it was just as well: there would have been no recognising the face. Stan Vargo had been no picture in life, but death had not been kind to him. It had been a savage fall, head-first on to the rocks. Even from the boat the sight was horrible. Both Sprat and Peter Polmean turned away, and emptied their stomachs into the sea.

Half-a-leg and Denzil exchanged glances. 'Come on,' Half-a-leg said, as they came up to shallow water short of the rock. 'No time

285

to be squeamy. We'll have the tide turning on us directly. Peter, you come out here with the painter. It's still a bit deep, mind. Don't let her go. Sprat, you stay there and keep her steady. We two'll go.'

It was no easy matter. The lower rocks were slippery with weed – they were under-water half the tide – and the body was lying inaccessibly. Denzil's good suit was caked with mud in a moment and his shoes – not made for climbing – were soaked through. But desperation lends strength, and they managed it at last. Half-a-leg took the head and Denzil the legs, and between them they carried the broken body towards the boat, now firmly grounded by the last ebbing of the tide.

Before they reached it, though, Half-a-leg stopped. 'Poor kids,' he said, nodding towards the two still with the boat. He stripped off his battered jumper. 'Put this over the head, shall us? Save them the worst, any rate.'

'You told the police?' Denzil asked suddenly, as they covered the battered face.

'Oh Lor',' Half-a-leg said. 'Never thought of un. Better had, I suppose, when we get back.' They hoisted the body into the boat.

After that no one said anything for a long time. They worked together – the tide turning under them – until they were out past the point. And then it was Sprat who said,

'Look! Over there! There's someone in the water. In trouble, from the look of it.'

And, still bearing their grisly cargo, they rowed out to help.

Tom and Olivia alighted from the horse-bus at the top road, but Olivia refused to take the short-cut over the stile to the Cove. 'Too steep and slippery,' she said tearfully, and Tom had to lead her around the long way by the road. Even then, she was not used to walking on hills, and she almost turned her ankle. Tom took the opportunity to slip his arm around her, and she leaned on him gratefully.

'I'm a fool, Tom,' she said breathlessly. 'What am I doing here? And dragging you away from the shop. What will Mr White say?'

Tom had been asking himself the same question. It seemed much less excusable somehow, now that he was actually here. But there was nothing for it now.

'There he is, look,' he said, pointing to the beach. 'Your precious Denzil Vargo. And what did I tell you? There's that girl of his.'

'What are they doing?'

'Taking a boat out, by the look of it.'

'I don't believe it,' Olivia said, her voice high-pitched with disbelief. 'He walks out of the office, leaves me, leaves my father, says nothing at all about it, and goes *boating*!'

Tom couldn't improve on that, so he said nothing.

'Well,' Olivia said, 'I shall have something to say about that!' She began to hurry down the hill. It was foolish, because she lost her footing, and if Tom had not seized her in his arms she would have fallen.

'Olivia!' he said, pressing her close to him. 'Leave it. He is not worth your attention.' He sighed. 'If only...'

'What?'

'I was going to say, if only you had consented to marry me...' There, he had said it. And she didn't recoil.

She dropped her eyes. 'Perhaps it is not too late. I told Mr Vargo this morning that I would release him, if he wished.'

Tom's heart was thumping. He could hardly believe his good fortune. Or not so much fortune, he thought to himself: he had worked hard for this moment. 'And what did he say?'

She sighed. 'That is the problem. He said nothing. Asked me to meet him at the office and then – like I told you – when I went, he wasn't there!' She was crying again. He hated that.

He offered her a handkerchief, as he had once offered it to Sprat. 'Don't let tears spoil that pretty face.'

She looked at him. 'Pretty? No one has ever called me pretty. Not even Denzil.'

'Then he's blind as well as stupid,' Tom said, and his heart was singing. Mr Denzil Vargo, I have beaten you now.

'I shall tell him,' Olivia cried. 'Tell him that it is over between us. How dare he treat me in this way!' She tugged at Tom's arm. 'Come on.'

He couldn't argue with that, and he hurried with her down the hill to the beach. There was a woman on the path, and she turned eagerly to greet them.

'Come to lend a hand, have you? That's some good of you. Only you're too late, look. They're gone.' She gestured to the beach, where the rowers were already pulling away from the shore. 'Shame that is. Young fellow like you, be more use than that Nicholls girl – though it's good of her, too, turning out to help a Vargo.'

'She's not his cousin, then?' Tom said, not missing a trick.

She shook her head. 'Not she. Might have been, though, if my brother-in-law Billy'd had his way.'

'I'm sorry,' Olivia said, recollecting herself. 'You are...?'

'I'm Mary Vargo,' the woman said. 'Wife to 'im who went over the cliff. Leastways that's what we think. Some fool gave him money, and of course he went drinking with it. Left the public house reeling, and never came home. Lost his way in a stupor, looks like – and now...' She pressed a hand to her mouth and shook her head tearfully. 'Monster he was, but you wouldn't 'ave wished him this.'

Olivia said slowly, 'You are Mrs Vargo? Denzil's mother?'

The woman smiled then, a wan, proud smile. 'He's a good boy, Denzil. How that Stan ever fathered him, I don't know. He's gone out now, best suit and all, to try to bring back the body – after the way his father treated him and everything.'

Olivia was staring at her. 'Body? You mean he might be dead? Denzil's father?'

The woman looked at her pityingly. 'You fall over that cliff, my lover, you don't bounce. No, he's dead all right, whoever he is. Well, it's no good standing here. My neighbours'll be worrying what's happened. They've been up half the night with me as it is. Take them a couple of hours to bring it back – I'll slip back then, see them come home.' She shook her head. 'Want to come back for a cup of tea, do 'ee?'

'No, thank you,' Tom said, anxious to see her go. All that propaganda for Denzil could undo his hard work in a twinkling. Indeed, Olivia already looked stricken. 'Well,' he said, when the woman had gone, 'you see now what you have avoided. That could have been your mother-in-law. That un-educated creature.'

But Olivia wasn't listening. 'Oh, Tom. What have I done?' She was shaking from head to foot.

He held her again. 'You haven't done anything.'

She pulled away. 'Yes I have. Oh, Tom. It was me. I gave him the money. Denzil said I shouldn't, but I did. He told me he was starving and I believed him. Tom, I've got to go there. No, no, don't try to stop me – I must, I must.'

She was sobbing hysterically, and she flung herself away from him, down the beach.

Tom followed helplessly. 'Well, what are you going to do about it? Look at them, they're right out there at sea. Listen, Olivia, this is not your fault. You were just being your own generous self. It's not your fault the man kills himself. Always was a drunkard, everyone knows that.'

She stopped. 'Yes,' she said, more calmly, 'Denzil knew. And if I'd listened to him, none of this would have happened. I'm going after him.' She began tugging a little boat towards the water.

'Olivia, listen! Listen to me.'

She was still half crying. 'I shouldn't have listened to you in the first place. Now you can row, can't you, Tom, because if you can't I'll go after him myself.'

'Of course I can row,' Tom said. After all,

he'd done it before. 'Well, get in then. I don't know what good it'll do, but I'll take you after him, if that's what you want.' He was losing ground by sounding irritable, and he added, more gently, 'I told you, Olivia, anything for you.'

He rolled up his trousers and pushed the boat well afloat, and then scrambled in. The oars were already in it, and he put them in the oar-things, feeling very masculine.

It was easier than he expected. Much easier. The boat was moving out to sea almost without his having to do anything, except steer round a cork-and-barrel mooring occasionally. Must be the tide, Tom thought lazily. It was almost pleasurable until they got outside the Cove, where there was a little wind blowing, and choppy little waves began bouncing the boat.

Olivia was holding the sides. 'Other way,' she said. 'Over there, beyond the point!' and Tom dutifully circled, using one oar (he had seen Pincher do this), and began pulling in the other direction. But he was making no progress. The more he rowed, the more he drifted back in the direction he had come.

'Tom, what are you doing?' Olivia said. She leaned forward and seized an oar.

'Let go, you silly—' but he never finished the epithet. In his effort to wrest it from her, the oar-handle slipped from his grasp and began floating away. He leaned over to get it, but it was beyond his grasp. He was panicking now. He hauled the other oar aboard and knelt up, rocking. If he used the other oar he could reach it ... just...

Perhaps he would have done, if it wasn't for the wave. It pitched the boat upwards and Tom, leaning awkwardly at full stretch, lurched over the side and into the water. The cold hit him like a moving train. 'Olivia!'

But she was drifting away from him, paddleless. He could see her in the boat, kneeling up, her mouth screaming, 'Oh Tom! Tom! Help! Someone help!!' But the wind carried her voice away.

He couldn't swim, but the oar was floating. He clung to it desperately, but the more he struggled to clutch it the more it bobbed him under. His lungs were full of water, and his shoes were dragging him down. He was drowning. He was going to die – and it was all that Vargo's doing.

He was going down for the second time when a strong arm grasped him. Half-a-leg Roberts. Tom half recognised the man. With the desperation of the drowning he reached out, struggling, grasping, kicking.

'Stop it, you fool, you'll have me over too. Denzil, give me a hand here.'

And then Vargo's face. Tom lifted his own, and knew no more.

Denzil had drawn back his fist and, with

the pent-up anger of years, landed a punch under his chin that had knocked him senseless. Then with Half-a-leg he had dragged the unresisting body aboard.

When Tom came hazily to himself he was lying safely on the shore and Bullivant, of all people, was leaning over him.

Tom groaned, and closed his eyes again.

Three

It was a foregone conclusion, really, that Mr Bullivant would give chase, once he had been alerted by his wife.

She had telephoned the motor garage from the post office, as Denzil discovered later, to tell him the alarming news. Their daughter had been seen in tears, by an acquaintance, first being embraced in broad daylight, and then boarding the horse-bus for Penvarris in the company of a young man.

'Just walked out with her,' the woman had said, 'and in the middle of serving me too.'

The garage manager had offered his coach and pair, and it had not taken them long to follow. But by the time Denzil staggered ashore, exhausted from the exertion of rowing miles more than he'd bargained for, there was no need to offer explanations. Half the Cove and more than half Penvarris were waiting on the harbour wall, with conflicting explanations of their own.

'That's him,' Norah Roberts was announcing, pointing to Tom's inert figure in the boat. 'Cuddling and canoodling up there on the road like I don't know what. And that's the girl there, in the boat they're towing.'

'Denzil!' his mother detached herself from the crowd and ran towards him. He tried to go to her, but the strain of the last few hours was too much and he was forced to sit down on a stone before he fell in the shallows.

'Yes,' he said wearily. 'It's him. There, in the back of the boat.' He reached out a hand, and they comforted each other wordlessly, not for the fact but for what might have been. Meanwhile Half-a-leg and some of the other men were dragging the boat in and unloading her other passengers, dead and alive.

Half-a-leg scooped up the soaked and trembling Olivia and carried her ashore. She was shaking so much with fright and cold that a dozen women were around her in an instant, offering hot cups of tea and blankets. 'Half drowned, poor lamb!'

'What's she doing out there anyway?' someone said, and Denzil saw Bullivant shoulder his way through the crowd. Relief and anger fought for precedence on his face.

'I might ask the same question, young lady. What is the meaning of this?'

Olivia's shuddering was made worse by her sobs.

'Making a spectacle of us all,' her father

raged. 'You, a respectably brought-up girl, cavorting on the streets like a common harlot.' He *was* roused, Denzil thought. Such a word was not usually in his vocabulary. 'And then frightening us half to death by attempting to drown yourselves in a rowboat. As well you are engaged to be married to him. We shall have to bring the ceremony forward, that is all.'

Olivia let out a little bleat, and Denzil got to his feet, swaying. 'Excuse me, sir.'

Bullivant turned to him. 'And as for you, young man, I don't know whether to thank you for saving my daughter's life or have you horsewhipped for bringing her here.'

Denzil took a step towards him. 'Mr Bullivant. It is true that I left the office without permission, but I didn't bring Olivia here. I came to fetch my father's body home. She came with Tom Courtney, there in the boat. I had to knock him out, I'm afraid, to rescue him. He would have sunk the lot of us, else.'

Bullivant's face spoke of his shock, though no words came.

'Told 'ee that before,' Norah said, folding her arms stoutly. 'Said it was him lying in the boat. Saw them with me own eyes. Seen that Courtney boy before, I have, down here pestering Sprat Nicholls.'

'As to the engagement, Mr Bullivant, Olivia has done me no dishonour. Only this morning, before we left for the office, she informed me that she wished to be released.'

Bullivant's scowl deepened. 'She released you, for that scoundrel?'

Denzil sighed. 'Both of us, sir, had affections elsewhere, I think.' He became suddenly aware of the crowd of watching eyes. Even the arrival of the corpse could not compare with this spectacle – Olivia's look of wretched humiliation and his own spoiled, dripping suit. 'Now if you will excuse me, I must look to my father.'

'And if I may suggest, Mr Bullivant sir, I'll fetch some dry clothes for the lady? I have some that might fit her, until she can reach her own.' Sprat was suddenly beside them, looking at Denzil with eyes that shone with hope.

He was shivering with cold and tiredness, but he bent towards her.

'Denzil ... not here! Everyone's looking.'

'I thought you loved me.'

'I do, but...'

'Then shut up and come and kiss me. Who cares what people think? We've listened to them for far too long as it is.'

And as he took her in a damp embrace, and she lifted her salty, shivering lips to his, Wilhemina Nicholls – her heart soaring with the seagulls – could only close her eyes and agree.

Epilogue

The marriage of Olivia Bullivant and Thomas Courtney was a very hushed affair. Only a very few relatives and friends attended. Claude Emms was there, scarlet-faced in a tight suit, and Mr White from the Emporium – who had offered Tom a rise in honour of his marriage. And, of course, Denzil Vargo from the shipping office and his own new bride, who had been married even more quietly the week before.

Olivia's wedding bonnet was hand-made for the occasion by the young Mrs Vargo, and very handsome it was too – though not as handsome as the one Mrs Bullivant wore, a year later, for the christening of her first grandchild. That Wilhemina Vargo had a real talent for hats. Everybody said so – some of her designs were even sent to London, though she never showed the least desire to go back there herself.

Of course – as Norah Roberts told the baker – that girl had always been a wild one. Rowing boats, and working for the suffragists. Even went with them on that Cornish

299

march – made a large hat on purpose, trimmed with purple, green and white, the colours of the movement. Said she had to do it, in memory of a friend. While that poor Olivia Courtney learned to smile again by tending to her child, like a respectable person, Sprat Vargo was standing on a soapbox. Her husband didn't even seem to mind – he always did indulge her in everything.

Well, what could you expect? A Cove girl wedded to an up-overer! And her parents were as thrilled with him as she was. They had got too mighty for the Cove these days themselves. Moved into that little cottage up Penvarris that Denzil was rumoured to be keeping up – all repainted and refurnished, if you ever heard the like – for his mother. Of course, he was made up to be a manager now, and the Bullivants had been generous when he wed.

Yes, it seemed to be working out wonderful, Norah had to admit it, Mrs Vargo Senior looking after the three of them. Course, Pincher was the same as ever, coming down to his pots, and Myrtle wasn't as well as she might be and couldn't really manage on her own, but she still had a sharp tongue on her and she held court up there, asking Mrs Polmean and people up for tea like as if she was royalty! Though it was a nice little cottage inside, Norah had to admit, and they kept it lovely.

And they were a handsome couple, the young Vargos. You couldn't really grudge them. Perhaps there'd be a child one of these days, put a stop to her daft political tricks. In the meantime, they were doing well. Apparently he was a stalwart at the office – Bullivant was always saying how he couldn't do without him – and she was a real magic hand with hats.

It was only a pity that the dreadful war should happen and so many of the hats she made were black.